EMPOWERING ANTOINETTE

M.E. Rodriguez

authorHOUSE®

AuthorHouse™
1663 Liberty Drive
Bloomington, IN 47403
www.authorhouse.com
Phone: 1 (800) 839-8640

Published by AuthorHouse   04/29/2017

ISBN: 978-1-5246-7221-8 (sc)
ISBN: 978-1-5246-7220-1 (e)

Library of Congress Control Number: 2017902383

Print information available on the last page.

Dedication

I dedicate this book to that special person who taught me to dream big, who empowered me with her love and wisdom, and who by her own acts of courage taught me strength of character.

Thank you, Mother, this book is for you!

Contents

Prologue

Fifteen years ago, Antoinette shivered in the corner of the pitch-black room, tears streaming from her eyes as she choked her worn-out teddy bear. Her body was very sore. She hated the nighttime because that is when he'd come to her in a drunken stupor. This time he'd nearly killed her. She pushed the sobs into the belly of her bear to muffle the sounds from the pain, fearing she would wake the monster snoring on her bed.

It was her twelfth birthday, and she wanted to run far, far away. Sadie, Antoinette's secret companion hidden deep within the recesses of her mind, had helped her plan the great escape. But their plan didn't work. She had gotten caught. Now she had to pay the price, as she had many times before since her mother's death. She thought of her mother often during times like this. She was named after her. The fading memory of her mother's love and protection could barely comfort her now. Antoinette had been too young when her mother died. She knew the monster had something to do with it. Sadie had told her so. Her imaginary friend was tough on her and blatantly truthful, but Antoinette knew that she was just trying to protect her. No one else could.

"You stupid little girl." Antoinette could remember hearing Sadie laughing at her inside her mind as she spoke those words, the words that tonight echoed in Antoinette's memory. And although she hadn't wanted to hear it, Sadie explained in detail how the monster violently raped her mother after she had caught him fondling Antoinette. His shame fueled his anger, and he beat her to death. Internal bleeding killed her. *He* killed her. Because he was the sheriff, he knew how to make her death seem like a random act of violence. He dumped her body that very same night. Her murder was never solved, and no one ever dared to question the sheriff about it. Antoinette had told Sadie she was lying, but now she knew it was the truth. Sobbing ferociously into her bear, she related to her mother's disgrace now more than ever.

Finally overcome with searing pain, Antoinette fainted into unconsciousness. Moments later, her eyes opened wide. But it wasn't Antoinette anymore; it was Sadie. Her imaginary friend had transcended beyond the limits of pretend and had entered reality. The alter personality awoke and would now take control of the situation.

"Don't worry," Sadie whispered into Antoinette's mind as she took over the child's near-dead body. Sadie was stronger than Antoinette, and she would kill the bastard for what he had done. Not feeling the pain from the abuse Antoinette had just been dealt, Sadie dropped Teddy as she quietly tiptoed out of the room and down the stairs to the living room. Silently, she searched the dark room for his gun, eventually spying it on the end table next to his favorite chair. She knew it was loaded because it always was. Then she returned to her room to send the son of a bitch to damnation.

Standing at the end of the bed, she looked down at the monster and cocked the gun. To her surprise, he woke at the sound of the gun setting. In startled astonishment, he angrily shouted, "Antoinette, what in God's name are you doing?"

"I am Sadie, you bastard. Go to hell," she yelled. Then she pulled the trigger, killing Antoinette's father in her bed. Sadie dropped the gun as she passed out on the floor.

Padre Alvaro was shocked when he saw Antoinette walk toward him. The small-town priest suddenly felt sick when he saw the girl's bloodstained gown. She was acting odd. He knew something terrible must have happened, so he rushed toward her, calling for help. Antoinette collapsed at his feet.

The turmoil from the ambulances and police left Padre Alvaro exhausted. Quietly, he sat in his favorite worn-out leather chair. *What to do?* he thought. Two crimes had been committed and, ironically, both perpetrators had become victims. As he sighed, he noticed a wall plaque in the corner of the room. It had been a gift from his sister, a reminder of God's Ten Commandments.

Getting up from his chair, he went over to study the orders given by God through Moses. Slowly, he read each one. Stopping at the fifth commandment, he quietly repeated the opening words, "Thou shall honor thy father and mother." *But what of incest?* he wondered. He read the sixth commandment that followed, "Thou shall not kill," and thought of the coincidence of Antoinette's situation. A big moral dilemma hung heavy in the priest's mind. *Could a child really be held accountable for murder if she was being physically violated? Should one be forced to honor an abusive parent under such circumstances?*

"Christ," he whispered. *The child probably doesn't even realize what she has done. She needs help, not punishment,* he concluded, remembering the state of shock Antoinette had been in when the ambulance drove her away. He picked up the phone and began to dial.

"St. Anne's Orphanage. May I help you?" said a nun in a gentle voice.

"Yes, Sister. My name is Padre Alvaro. I am calling to speak with the child psychiatrist, Dr. Ceci Ingles. Is she available?"

"Oh, I'm so sorry, Padre. She is on vacation until next week. Shall I leave her a message?" the sister offered. The priest left his name and telephone number with the nun, stressing his urgency to speak with the psychiatrist. Hanging up the phone, he contemplated his plan to help Antoinette.

The crowd outside the sheriff's house was growing. No one could believe that their own sheriff had been murdered. Not knowing the circumstances provoking the crime, everyone's response was more or less the same: "Not the sheriff! What a decent man he seemed to be—and a good father, raising that child on his own. You know, he never did remarry."

Awe, not disgust, was the opinion of the day, Detective Quesada sarcastically thought while reviewing the day's events on his drive home. He understood, however, that men like the sheriff were never what you'd expect them to be. Seventeen years on the force had taught him a thing or two, and quite frankly, he couldn't help but think how lucky the bastard was for having gotten killed. A child-molesting sheriff would never have fared well in prison. Pulling up into his driveway, Detective Quesada sat in his car for a few moments, realizing how fortunate he was. He had a beautiful wife, and a daughter who had twisted his heart around her precious little finger. *Bastard,* he thought, as he got out of the car and went inside his home.

The following week proved to be frustrating for the police and deeply saddening for Padre Alvaro. The damage Antoinette had suffered was extensive. Unable to talk, she remained in a suspended state between life and death. Fearing her fragility, all who cared for her prayed for God's mercy. The police had an open-and-shut case, but for legal reasons they needed to talk to her. The crime was an obvious case of self-defense, but the law was the law and proper procedure had to be followed. It was a murder, after all— and a murder of a sheriff was no light matter.

Padre Alvaro sighed, sipped on his cognac, and contemplated Antoinette's situation. *Could this child possibly have the strength to survive the abuse? Would she ever be able to live a normal, healthy life with normal, healthy relationships?* "Only time will tell," Padre Alvaro whispered as he took down the last of the cognac in a swallow. Turning out the light, he chuckled at the irony of his words. Time, not God, seemed to be the only force at hand.

Chapter 1

The Rescue

P adre Alvaro prayed for Antoinette several hours each day. Sometimes when she was awake, he'd hold her hand and pray out loud, hopeful she would hear him and know she was safe. Sometimes doubtful she could hear him at all, he just offered silent prayers from his heart. "For many, life was not fair", he thought as he searched his faith for the right spiritual answer. This time the answer was not so apparent to him. He was angry at her father, and at God for allowing this to happen. "For the kingdom of heaven belongs to them," he whispered sarcastically. "But must a twelve-year-old child suffer through hell before she gets there?" He challenged his teachings and searched his soul for enlightenment.

The LPN on duty popped her head into Antoinette's room to inform the priest, "Padre, there is a call for you at the nurse's station." Knowing it must be the psychiatrist, he quickly went to answer the call.

"Ceci? Oh, thank God you got through to me." The priest explained the events of the week and his hopes that Ceci would work with Antoinette. He had worked with

1

Ceci in the past and knew that if anyone was able to see Antoinette through this personal tragedy, it was her. She agreed, promising to look in on the child Monday once she returned to work.

Padre Alvaro hoped that Ceci would agree to have Antoinette admitted to the orphanage. There appeared to be no next of kin, so at least at the orphanage she would have the loving care of the nuns. He had dedicated two years of service at the institute prior to receiving his own congregation. It was much more than an orphanage; it was an educational center and a place for healing. Most of the children were placed in good loving Catholic homes and the ones who weren't still fared better in life after leaving the place.

Returning to Antoinette's room, Padre Alvaro encountered Dr. Falzo performing tests. Antoinette was unresponsive. The doctor motioned to the priest that he wanted to speak with him outside the room. In the hallway, Padre Alvaro listened carefully as Dr. Falzo explained, "Antoinette is in a very delicate state right now but she will heal from the physical injuries. We have stopped the bleeding and the hymeneal and urethral injuries will heal. She has been given antibiotics to prohibit infection. There *is* a chance that she may never be able to have children, this is not the first time this young girl has been raped." With a shift in his stance and clearing of his throat he continued, "She is in shock, and given her circumstance, it is understandable. It will take a much longer period, however, for her to deal with her issues on an emotional level. We will keep her under observation a little while longer and then move her to the children's psych ward for monitoring and short term rehabilitation." The priest thanked the doctor for his explanation and then returned to the room to pray before he left for the day. Later that evening, Antoinette was moved to the psych ward to begin her long journey of recuperating.

Chapter 2

The Recovery

As she had promised, Ceci looked in on Antoinette upon her return from vacation and ran some basic tests. It was apparent that the child's survival mechanism had taken over and she was not ready to face reality. "Reality," Ceci said, harrumphing to herself, understanding the long road toward recuperation that lay before the young girl. This was Ceci's expertise as a psychiatrist, though she never could get over the initial disgust she felt when thinking of the abuse her patients suffered. She knew, however, that those patients needed her very much, so she focused her attention on the beautiful little girl before her.

Ceci looked down at her patient, noting the red curly hair that crowned the child's still slightly bruised, porcelain-looking skin. One barely noticed the speckled flecks across her nose. She noticed Antoinette's cut lip was healing quit well and there was barely a trace of swelling, thinking their fullness was meant to outline a big, beautiful smile. Sighing, Ceci knew this little girl had not had a reason to smile in a very, very long time. Sadly, she knew that the girl was starved for maternal affection. Though she doubted

Antoinette could hear her, she spoke to her young charge in soft tones, assuring her she was in safe hands and promising she would visit with her twice daily. Half an hour later, she left Antoinette and went to have a talk with Padre Alvaro.

"We must speak with Detective Quesada and go before the court to release Antoinette from the criminal court system so we can transfer her guardianship to the orphanage," Ceci said. Decisively, the priest called Detective Quesada and conversed about their intentions to have Antoinette admitted to the orphanage. Fortunately, the detective was in agreement with them and willingly offered his support, saying that he would go before the court.

During the following weeks, the criminal court declared that Antoinette had acted in self-defense, under a state of temporary insanity, and committed her to a psychiatric care center, the Institute for Mental Healing, owned by the orphanage. The orphanage was granted guardianship and now the case was closed for all except Antoinette. Young Antoinette, to whom God showed His mercy, had awoken during this time. Yet she remained steadfastly mute as she began a new journey.

Over the course of the month, Ceci visited Antoinette two times a day. They made small steps of progress. Although Antoinette wouldn't talk, she began to appear more alert and show facial expressions regarding her likes and dislikes. Ceci, feeling good about her patient's progress, admired the little girl's strength of character. Even Dr. Falzo had paid a visit and told her that Antoinette seemed to be healing well.

Noting her observations in her chart, Ceci froze at the sound coming from behind her. "Leave her alone," a husky voice warned.

Slowly, Ceci turned toward her patient and asked, "Antoinette?" The little girl looked at Ceci and pointed an accusatory finger at her.

"I said, leave her alone."

Ceci immediately recognized what was happening, recalling a similar reaction in a patient she had treated many years ago. "Who are you?" she pressed.

"Sadie."

"Where is Antoinette?"

"Safe. I'm not telling you. Leave her alone," she responded in a defensive, childish manner.

"I want to help her," Ceci baited.

"Go away!" Sadie screamed.

The doctor stopped her line of questioning. Antoinette turned her head and closed her eyes. Ceci knew she would remain unresponsive to her. She opened Antoinette's chart and noted the event:

> First verbal contact has been made with Antoinette, but through a second personality named Sadie. It would appear that Sadie is an alter persona of Antoinette that the latter had created to protect herself from the abuse she was suffering. It is unclear if other subpersonalities exist. Complete rehabilitation requires the cooperation of all alters. At this time, the Sadie personality is protective and very defensive. The revelation of her existence, however, is an important factor for structuring therapy, though I have not yet determined the

trigger for causing this side of Antoinette's personality to appear.

Ceci closed her chart, grabbed her briefcase, and left the room, thinking that she must talk to Padre Alvaro.

Chapter 3

The priest was astonished at Ceci's words. "My God," he slowly spoke. It was a situation he couldn't quite grasp.

Ceci continued her conversation with him, saying, "It actually is not an uncommon reaction among young children who are severely abused. The mind splits as a way of escaping from a painful reality. Children generally make reference to imaginary friends. Given this girl's background, with the loss of her mother and being raised by an abusive father, she survived only because she allowed the creation of this other personality. In other words, she allowed her imaginary friend to become '*real*.' Right now, Sadie is in control, but we are moving in the right direction, Padre. I understand this is difficult for you to comprehend, but she has responded and conversed with me, which is a very good sign."

Nodding his understanding, the priest quietly asked Ceci what he could do to help the girl.

"There isn't much you can do at this moment. I've got to work with Sadie to get her to trust me enough to allow me to talk with Antoinette. If we are lucky, she is the only alter. Rehabilitation will focus on getting all alters to let go so that only one main personality exists. It will take some time. Your prayers and your visits are the best gifts you can offer her. Also, since Antoinette is no longer in a physical crisis, we can structure a more intense rehabilitative program with the goal of eventually moving her from the Institute of Mental Health to permanent resident at the orphanage." The priest thanked the psychiatrist for her efforts and promised to visit Antoinette often. Stopping at the Institute's chapel before leaving, he silently offered a prayer of gratitude for Ceci's having taken charge of Antoinette's care.

The Institute was not unlike a hospital, with its own medical staff dedicated for mentally disturbed children. The specialist staff knew the distressing situations their children had experienced and took a holistic approach to healing. They also knew that the trauma would later reveal itself in all sorts of ways. Antoinette's situation was not new to them. Eventually her alter personalities would divulge a horrific story. Then time would be spent on getting her personalities to cooperate and eventually making them subservient to one main personality. Until this occurred, the Institute would be Antoinette's home.

Chapter 4

P ensively thinking about her next patient, Ceci sat in her office. Initially, communication with the Sadie persona had been a struggle for both therapist and patient. More often than not, Sadie was uncooperative and violent. Eventually, however, Ceci had been able to gain some of Sadie's trust, and the two of them were then able to move forward with the next phase of treatment. The succeeding two-hour play sessions three times a week had helped Ceci gain more of Sadie's confidence and provided the opportunity for Sadie to interact with the other girls on the ward. This was actually quite helpful. Yet only on a few occasions during the past four or five months had Sadie been willing to allow Ceci to have contact with Antoinette. These prime opportunities only occurred while Sadie was under hypnosis. During these few instances, Ceci could see a classic Gemini syndrome. Whereas Antoinette seemed likable yet timid, Sadie was bold and often mean-spirited.

Coming out of her reverie, Ceci checked her watch and realized she had just a few minutes to grab a cup of coffee before the nurse would bring her next patient. Knowing this session was with Sadie, Ceci silently hoped it would be "the" session that would bring Antoinette out of her shell. It was time that Antoinette began to show herself more willingly.

"Sadie, how are you today?" The doctor rose to greet her patient and lead her to the counseling area.

"Do you really care, or do they just train you to say that?" Sadie answered in her usual defensive tone, plopping herself in the all too familiar chair.

"Well, I can see we are having a rough day. And yes, unfortunately for you, I do care. I care very much," Ceci rallied back while sitting herself into a comfortable chair facing her patient. She had set up this part of her office like a living room, making the sessions more comfortable for everyone.

"Why?" The doctor could feel the child's direct hard stare. It was a chilling look that made her uncomfortable. Sadie seemed to know this and to enjoy the effect she had on her therapist.

"Well, for many reasons, but why don't we start by you telling me what's bugging you?" Ceci asked, wanting to redirect the conversation.

"You bother me, these sessions bother me, and I want to leave this place." Sadie was agitated and spoke in a loud voice. Feeling angry today, she wanted everyone she met to feel the same way.

"Where would you go, Sadie?" The child couldn't stand Ceci's calmness. As much as she tried, she just couldn't provoke her. "Sadie, where would you go?" the doctor asked again.

"Well, obviously, I wouldn't be telling you now, would I?!"

Ceci kept quiet for a moment, looking at the anger that distorted the child's facial expression. Even so, the little girl was adorable, like a fragile porcelain doll, no matter what bullying nonsense came out her mouth. Ironically, Ceci thought, she always clutched her teddy, an action that just didn't seem to fit Sadie's personality.

"What's bothering you, Sadie?" the doctor asked a third time, ignoring the child's biting responses.

"I don't feel like talking about it." Sadie folded her arms and put on her best pout.

"I've got a great idea, Sadie," Ceci said enthusiastically, trying her best to change the mood. The young girl ignored her. "How about we bust out of here and go shopping?" she continued, making some notes in her chart. That caught Sadie's attention. This was the first time Ceci had seen the girl soften. "While I get my things together and let the staff know of our plans, do me a favor, Sadie."

"Yeah, what?" she asked suspiciously. The therapist grabbed the sketch pad and colored pencils and placed them on the coffee table in front of the girl.

"Do me a favor and draw me a picture of yourself. It's a game we are going to play."

"But I can't draw!"

"Just do your best. I'll be back in a sec," Ceci explained nonchalantly as she headed toward the door, silently praying that her patient would do as she asked.

Sadie looked at the blank page for several minutes. Her sloppy appearance evidenced that she never really paid attention to her physical self. Noticing a reflective globe high on the wall, she slowly got up and went toward it. Looking up, Sadie stared at her reflection for several minutes as if in a daze. Who should she draw, the ugly girl in the foreground, the one with short black hair and black eyes, or the pretty girl in the background, the one with red curly hair and deep green eyes? Enraged, she returned to the sketch pad and began to draw. All too soon the uncontrollable hate welled inside her. She ripped out the page of her drawing and threw the crumpled ball at the reflective globe. Deciding then and there she wasn't going to play this game, she went into a fit, throwing everything within her grasp to the ground. She was ugly and angry, and she wanted everyone to suffer.

A few moments later, Ceci returned to find Sadie scolding the bear she had propped up into the corner of the chair. "You're a stupid, stupid little girl, Antoinette! You think you can hide from me?!" Suddenly the child began beating her bear, fist over fist.

"Sadie?" The child slowly turned and faced her therapist.

Ceci could see the rage play across Sadie's face. *Too much hostility for such a young child to possess,* she thought.

As if hearing but not seeing her therapist, the child turned and screamed. Yet Ceci remained still and didn't say another word. She let her vent. She did so until Sadie was overcome with exhaustion. Ceci returned to her chair and quietly, methodically began talking Sadie down. "You are okay, Sadie. What you are feeling is anger, and that is okay. I understand what happened to you and Antoinette, but you both are safe now. Look at me. I am here to help you, Sadie—you and Antoinette. You both are okay now."

Emotionally drained, the child returned to her seat and remained silent. *Maybe,* the psychiatrist thought with a hint of self-admonition, *it is too soon for her to be out in public.* Something had triggered Sadie into a rage. Ceci needed to know what it was if she was going to help her. The doctor got up from the chair, went to her desk, and opened a drawer with a key. Grabbing a chilled bottled water from the mini fridge, she gave Sadie a sedative. Unemotionally, the child took it. She was sweaty. In a motherly fashion, the doctor brushed the red curly locks from her little patient's face. Ceci, knowing that Sadie would rest now, called for the nurse to return the child to her room.

The nurse quietly coaxed Antoinette's cooperation. All the staff referred to her as Sadie, knowing her delicate situation. Ceci quietly sat in her office, ignoring the mess she had yet to pick up, and reflected on the event. "What set her off?" In pensive reflection, she caught sight of the crumpled ball of paper lying in the corner of the room by the wastebasket and got up to retrieve it. To her surprise, it was the drawing she had asked her patient to draw. But it didn't look like her. A drawing of a child with black untamed hair and black eyes void of emotion stared back at Ceci. *No,* Ceci realized, *this is Sadie, at least the best as Antoinette can represent her. The red scribble on the bottom of the page must represent blood.* It was a rudimentary drawing of the grotesque event, her rape.

Chapter 5

Ceci squinted and rubbed her temples. She was exhausted from analyzing the drawing; it was intense and meant several things. This child saw herself as a reflection of her father, a man with dark hair and eyes. *She identifies with the very man she* hates, *yet probably loved because he was the only family she had really known.* "The thin line between love and hate," she whispered. It was then that she realized she had been remiss, failing to take into account the emotional impact that the actual murder had had on the child.

What was the depth of this child's hatred? Ceci had handled Antoinette's therapy as if she were simply a rape victim, but Antoinette was a rape victim and a murderer—shame and guilt compounded by intense hatred. "Unforgivable, Ceci," the doctor said, quietly scolding herself while picking up the tornado mess her patient left behind. *What makes a person cross the line to commit murder? What extent of abuse must have existed to force this child to cross that line? The fact that she committed murder separates Antoinette from all the other girls.* Looking back at the child's drawing, Ceci now understood that the blood in the picture was Antoinette's father's blood and not her own blood from being viciously violated. The Sadie persona hated herself for what she had done as much as she hated the man she had murdered, so she portrayed herself as him in her drawing.

Too tired to continue her analysis, Ceci closed the folder, and began the routine for closing the office.

Turning the key to the medicine drawer, she heard a soft knock on the door. Grabbing her purse, she turned off the light and headed out. To her surprise, Padre Alvaro was waiting patiently outside. "Oh, Padre, I didn't expect you!"

"A bad moment?"

"Oh no, just I … I just thought it was one of the nurses, that's all. How can I help you?"

"Nothing really. I just came from Antoinette's room and thought to check in on you. You must be exhausted, I know, but I thought you might want to get a bite to eat."

Ceci sighed and realized she hadn't had anything except a cup of coffee before her visit with Antoinette. Yeah, food sounded good. "Why not?" she agreed, closing the office door. In a sincere, gentlemanly fashion, Padre Alvaro escorted his guest down the hall.

"The oven-baked pizza is their specialty," he suggested. "And the house cabernet sauvignon is very good." Indifferent to the menu, Ceci agreed to the priest's suggestion. She was preoccupied and he sensed it, knowing a little bit of what had gone on from the other nurses. "I hear you had a tough day." Ceci just smirked.

The waiter brought their glasses of wine. Ceci took a gulp. "I'm sorry, Padre. Not very ladylike, I suppose." He chuckled and tried his best to lighten the mood with a corny joke. She laughed, at first politely, and then uncontrollably as the stress flowed from her body.

Wiping the tears from her eyes, she said, "That's the dumbest joke I've ever heard!" He knew, dumb as it was, that the laughter had done her well.

"On a more serious note," Ceci said, "I know Antoinette has to climb Mount Everest, so to speak. I know I have to be her guide. But what I don't understand, Padre—and forgive me for my lack of comprehension—is why you are so devoted to this child. I don't understand because we have had many abused children in our care but you've been particularly attentive to Antoinette. Mind you, she does need and deserve it, but can you clarify this for me?"

The priest sat looking pensively at his friend. She looked vulnerable. "Ceci, Antoinette came to me, remember? I've not had that experience before. Her hope was found in me, I suppose. I cannot fail her." Ceci looked at the priest as if she were seeing him for the first time as a man. Like him, she was becoming too emotionally involved with Antoinette. Silently, she promised to detach herself from this patient. Just then, the pizza arrived, interrupting her private thoughts.

"Oh my God, this is good!" she exclaimed on her first bite, not realizing how hungry she really was.

"I told you!" He relished the moment.

After their meal, he ordered two espressos without asking her if she wanted one.

"I'll be up all night!"

"I'm sure you won't. Looks like you're in dire need of a good night's rest. I'm sorry I kept you out so late." Ceci waved his concern away and commented that she hoped she didn't look that bad. He thought she looked beautiful.

After paying the bill, Padre Alvaro scooted out of the booth and offered his elbow to escort the doctor out. Ceci took his arm as they left the restaurant while the other customers curiously watched as they left.

Chapter 6

Ceci checked her watch; Sadie was late. Today she had planned an important session with hopes of bringing the Antoinette persona to the forefront. Just as she reached for the phone to call the nurse's station, her patient strolled in. In her typically arrogant fashion, Sadie offered no excuse for being late. Plopping herself into the chair, she hissed, "Psychoanalyze me!"

"No. Antoinette, you missed your appointment. You must reschedule."

Shocked and suspicious, Sadie remarked, "Wrong patient. I'm Sadie, remember?"

"Quite frankly, Sadie, you are not progressing, so I can't do much for you. I've tried to speak with Antoinette, but you won't let me. I do not know why I am wasting my time, particularly when you, Sadie, think you can show up late and do as you please! The buck stops here. You've missed your appointment; it will have to be rescheduled." Ceci returned to her next patient's file, praying that Sadie would take the bait.

"You bitch! Whatever! I didn't want to see you anyway!"

"Sounds like something your father would say," Ceci flatly and purposely remarked.

"What do you know? You know nothing about him!" Sadie was furious. *How dare she!* she thought.

"Only that Antoinette loved him."

"Nonsense, you stupid bitch. He hurt her!"

"Yeah, he did, but she loved him, something you don't know anything about."

"I protected her. I loved her enough to kill the bastard!" Sadie's eyes turned dark, the all too familiar look of anger written across her face.

"Sadie, you may have thought you were protecting her then, but murder is not an easy solution to live with. Now you hide her, but she needs help. She needs to stop feeling guilty for what you've done. You've got to stop being so angry with Antoinette's father. He is gone now, so you've got to let it go. But you won't, Sadie. Because of this, I can't help you. But I can help Antoinette. If you love her, you'll let me talk to her. Until then, you must reschedule our appointment." Lying, Ceci added, "I have other people in the same circumstance who want help."

"Fine, you fucking bitch. We don't need you anyway!" Sadie screamed. Then she stood up to leave the room, slamming the door to the doctor's office on her way out.

The doctor wanted to cry, but instead she took deep breaths and focused on a gift Padre Alvaro had given her when she agreed to help Antoinette. The plaque included one of Mother Teresa's famous quotations about the selfish and evil nature of human beings: "You must love them anyway." Ceci read the words aloud, amazed by the strength that this woman had possessed. She wasn't sure if she could be that strong.

Chapter 7

S adie slammed the door to her room and fell onto the bed to cry out her anger. She loved Ceci, but now she was rejected by her doctor. No one was going to control her anymore. She wouldn't stand for it. Everyone was too nice in this place, and she hated them for it. However, today her therapist hadn't been nice, and it hurt—real bad. How could Ceci accuse Sadie of not protecting and loving Antoinette?! She didn't know a damn thing about it. Antoinette's father deserved to be dead. Sadie hated him. It was his fault; he'd made her do it. It wasn't her fault. She was furious that she was being accused of doing something wrong. In a fit of rage, she got up from the bed and tore her room apart, venting her hatred toward her father, herself, and Ceci. Exhausted, she crawled into bed and cried herself to sleep.

"Don't worry, little one," Antoinette mentally spoke to the Sadie alter. "It will be okay. You have saved me. But I must talk to Ceci now so I can save you." Antoinette's personality took control over the exhausted Sadie persona. With no physical signs on her body of the tantrum Sadie had thrown a short time ago, Antoinette got up from the bed and went to the mirror. She decided to change her outfit. *Sadie has no fashion sense,* she thought. Moments later, she was in a pink sundress and sandals. Satisfied, Antoinette grabbed her teddy and walked out the door to reschedule her appointment. She could feel the attention she drew as she walked by the nurse's station. They all complimented her outfit, evidently amazed at the child's sudden change.

Antoinette walked into the doctor's office in a familiar fashion. Ceci, her back to the door, was studying her next patient's file. Sensing someone behind her, she turned her chair, stopping when she saw Antoinette. The silent pause seemed to last for an eternity.

The doctor noted the change in her patient's appearance and demeanor. The white sandals and pink flowered sundress were gifts from the head sister, Sister Catherine, but they had never been worn. Sadie refused to wear a dress. *This definitely is not Sadie,* Ceci thought, as she met the young girl's eyes. They were now a lighter shade of green. "Antoinette, how may I help you?"

"I've come to reschedule my appointment."

"Come, have a seat please." After escorting Antoinette to the counseling area, she said, "I'll be with you in a moment." Going back to her office, Ceci picked up the phone and dialed the receptionist so she could delay her next appointment, believing that giving her attention to Antoinette was more important. Then she returned to the counseling area, where she found Antoinette flipping through a magazine.

"I'm glad you came, Antoinette. You look very pretty." The child smiled self-consciously. Ceci led her back to the office and motioned for her to have a seat. "Okay, let's get started. Antoinette, do you know why you are here?"

"To make me better?" she sheepishly answered.

"Yes, Antoinette, that's correct. Do you know who Sadie is?"

Unsure of how to respond, Antoinette looked down, biting her lower lip as she struggled with the decision. Sadie was her secret. No one was supposed to know about Sadie, but she had made a mess of things and now everyone knew. She shouldn't have done what she did. Antoinette contemplated her secret friend's actions, knowing that Sadie had only been trying to protect her.

"Antoinette, do you know Sadie?" Ceci quietly asked again.

"Yes."

The cat was out of the bag so to speak, giving Ceci a concise direction. "So, you know I've been seeing Sadie for some time now?"

"Yes," Antoinette whispered.

"Do you know what we've talked about?"

"Yes."

"Where is Sadie now?"

"Sleeping." Antoinette did not look up once as she spoke.

"Antoinette, do you trust me?"

The girl remained silent for a time. Ceci watched the emotions play across her face.

"I'm not sure."

"A good honest answer, my dear. You are going to be just fine."

After scheduling her next appointment with Ceci, Antoinette returned to her room. Having decided that everything was going to be okay, she crawled into bed. Quickly she fell into a deep sleep.

Chapter 8

Beginning a New Life

"**M**y God, has it really been eight years?" Ceci was proud of the beautiful young woman who stood before her. Antoinette was ecstatic because she had been accepted to all three of the universities she had applied to. "I'm so proud of you!" Ceci wiped a sentimental tear from her eye. "Antoinette, you never cease to amaze me!"

Ceci had now known this fine young woman almost half of her life. She knew where Antoinette had come from and was familiar with the will she possessed to succeed. After all was said and done, Antoinette was only behind two years in school. She gave her counselor, and best friend, a great big hug and kiss on the cheek, promising to come back for her advice about which of the schools she should attend. In a motherly fashion, Ceci assured her that her own decision would be the right one. Then she laughed as her young friend sang a chorus of "I'm so good" before she left to give the news to the girls she dormed with.

Yes, Ceci thought, Antoinette is good. *As a matter of fact, she seems very good at everything.*

The time had come for Ceci to leave too. She reminisced about the years she had spent helping Antoinette get her life back. Sadie had finally let her talk to Antoinette. From that point on, the rehabilitation accelerated. Each alter was aware of the existence of the other, a fact that allowed Ceci to coach Antoinette into taking control over Sadie. Eventually Sadie disappeared altogether. Ceci truly hoped that she was dead and gone. One could never be 100 percent certain, however, but the odds were in Antoinette's favor. Antoinette, after all, was a strong-willed and competitive individual. She excelled in school and in sports, and was well-liked by her fellow students and her teachers.

Today, Antoinette was an exuberant personality, a woman who had learned to take control of her life. But Ceci remembered the shy little girl who had come to her when she refused to deal with Sadie any longer. Antoinette had put Sadie to sleep indefinitely, trading her anger for the love that the sisters offered. The sisters never mentioned her father since that day. Against conventional psychotherapy theory, Ceci chose to focus Antoinette's attention on the future, instead of on the past, and dedicated herself to building the child's self-esteem. Antoinette's self-discipline impressed everyone, even her.

Thoughtfully, Ceci wondered if Antoinette would eventually marry and—hopefully—be able to have children. This was a subject that she had not discussed much, as she had not yet shown any real interest in boys. Though she was friendly with everyone, she never referenced any desire to date a particular boy like the other girls did. Ceci reflected upon the fact that she herself had never married. She assumed that her need for children was fulfilled by her playing the surrogate role with all the children she had helped over the years. She was an independent person all right, but she wasn't entirely sure if that is what she wished for her young friend. She thought that maybe she should explore this issue with Antoinette before the latter headed off for college. "Oh, she'll be all right," Ceci said to herself, shaking off her concerns. "Your time has now come and you have much to do." Next month she would officially be retired.

At fifty-five, Ceci considered herself still to be young. She wished to at last fulfill a lifelong dream of traveling to each of the four corners of the earth. What an adventure it would be. Having planned her life well, now she had the means to pursue her dream and was young enough to enjoy it. Yet she would pursue her dream alone, her only regret. Her thoughts returned to Antoinette, hoping that the young woman would not find herself in this same predicament.

Ceci sighed. In a month she would close this chapter of her life forever. Saddened by the thought of leaving the family she had adopted at the orphanage, she thought about Padre Alvaro and decided to write him to inform him of Antoinette's good news. He had never lost contact with Antoinette and truly cared for her in a fatherly fashion. This was good for Antoinette, giving her a positive image of men and an understanding of what being a father truly meant. Hopefully, this image would enable the young woman to make wise decisions regarding the men in her life. Ceci sat down to write. Antoinette's graduation would be at the end of the month. She knew that Padre Alvaro would want to be there.

Everyone agreed the graduation was beautiful. Padre Alvaro suggested that the three of them go out for an early supper to celebrate. Ceci and the padre could barely contain their excitement when listening to Antoinette ramble on enthusiastically about her academic plans. She, with Ceci's help, had chosen the University of Texas because it offered the best educational program. Plus, she'd been awarded a scholarship that would just about cover her tuition if she kept her grades up. Antoinette planned to get a part-time job to make up the difference.

Padre Alvaro felt a tug at his heart thinking that *his* little girl was all grown up and leaving. He had often thought about having a family of his own, but doing so would require him to leave the church. Though more than once he had considered the possibility, God, for whatever reason, had kept him in his place. Padre Alvaro looked at his friend Ceci and was thankful for all the work she had done with Antoinette. He realized how special the therapist had become to his own life. These two women were his family. He knew that Ceci really loved Antoinette, probably more than she loved her other patients, he guessed. That was Antoinette, a lovable and beautiful ball of energy.

Drifting back to reality, Padre Alvaro said a special prayer on Antoinette's behalf. Then they all enjoyed each other's company as if it were the last time they would be together. "Don't be silly," Antoinette replied when the padre suggested that she would fall out of touch. She assured both of them that she would not disappear from their lives and promised to keep in contact with them.

At one point in the dinner, Ceci took the joyous opportunity to mention her plans to retire and travel to the four corners of the earth. Ecstatic, Antoinette proposed a toast. Padre Alvaro felt a second tug at his heart.

He had become endeared to Ceci through the years. Quite frankly, he enjoyed her company when he went to visit Antoinette and the other children at the orphanage. Although he hid his emotions, he believed that if he ever chose to leave the priesthood, Ceci would be the very person he would wish to marry. Her short dirty-blonde hair was a stark contrast to her large chocolate-brown eyes. He liked her petite athletic figure. She was an expert in her professional field and had a sense of humor that made just about everyone she met like her immediately. Padre Alvaro felt like he was losing his family.

Chapter 9

"Wow, four years have gone by so quickly," Antoinette mentioned to her college roommate. They laughed, remembering how excited and scared they had been when they first arrived at the university. It was Antoinette's first experience out on her own in the "real" world. She had heard many stories about it, both good ones and bad ones.

Antoinette had always known that she wanted to be a physical therapist. At the orphanage, there were many kids who benefited from physical therapy. She often volunteered to help them as well. She loved children, and she had a special way about her that caused them to love her back. Now she had accomplished her academic goal with the highest honors and had accepted a job at the Baptist Hospital in Miami, Florida. The pay was great and the cost of living bearable.

Packing her bags, she was disappointed that Ceci and Padre Alvaro had missed her graduation. Ceci was last known to be traveling throughout Asia. Antoinette smiled, knowing that her former therapist must be having the time of her life. But she was becoming concerned about Padre Alvaro. She had left several messages for him, but he had not returned her calls. That was very out of character for him. He'd never before missed any of the major events in her life. He did, however, send her a congratulations card from some place in Florida that mentioned he was on vacation.

"I'm heading for the sun and fun, my dear. May life treat you well. And let us always keep in touch." Antoinette hugged her roommate. She hated farewells. A taxi was waiting outside to take her to the airport.

Two hours later, Antoinette finally plopped into her assigned seat between an elderly woman and an oversized man. It seemed that everyone in the world was traveling, and the plane was overbooked. *In just a few more hours, I'll be out of this mess and on my way to Sister Catherine's home,* she silently reminded herself.

Sister Catherine had been old when Antoinette arrived at the orphanage, but she'd retained her sense of humor. She had finally retired a few years after Antoinette left for school. Having networked through the sisterhood before coming south, Antoinette found out that Sister Catherine, the former head nun, was living close to her new employer. The sister, who had been quite affectionate with Antoinette when she was at the orphanage, gladly opened her home to the new graduate until Antoinette found a place of her own. "Never look a gift horse in the mouth," Antoinette had said to herself, taking the sister up on her offer.

After the hugs and hellos, Sister Catherine showed Antoinette to her room. It was a comfortable place with its own bathroom. Feeling grateful, Antoinette returned to the kitchen table and sat to chat with her host, who hadn't changed a bit, she thought, as she laughed at one of her witty sayings. Sister Catherine was jolly as ever and seemed only slightly older. The two talked about the sister's retirement and how she had ended up in south Florida. She'd wanted to be near her brother, who recently had passed away. "Ah, a time comes for all of us when we must leave a place of comfort and walk down new paths that God has laid before us," the nun remarked. "And you, dear, you have grown up so well. You truly are beautiful. What plans do you have for this next chapter of your life?" Antoinette spoke of her new employment and her desire to find a place to call home. She didn't know much about south Florida and was grateful for the sister's help. "Not at all, my dear. You're young—what, twenty-four? Ah, you have your whole life ahead of you. Enjoy yourself!" Sister Catherine beamed as only a jolly old woman can do.

The two women reminisced while Sister Catherine made dinner and Antoinette set the table. Pot roast with potatoes, carrots, and onions was the main dish, accompanied by rice and a green bean salad. It was just the two of them, but there was enough food for at least six more guests. Reading Antoinette's thoughts, the sister remarked, "I was always told that it is better to have too much food than not enough 'cause you can always freeze the leftovers." Her roundish figure proved she liked to cook.

After cleaning up following the fine meal, Antoinette excused herself, saying that she was exhausted. Then she retired to her room.

Antoinette showered and crawled into bed. Exhausted but not yet sleepy, she lay there taking in the décor of her room. White ruffled curtains accented the beige and pink calico wallpaper. A serene feeling overcame her, and she nestled into her white goose-down comforter. *Life is good,* she thought before she drifted fast asleep.

Waking up early was Antoinette's usual routine, so she didn't mind the light that filled the room as the sun began to rise. The room was prettier in the morning, she thought. She casually got herself out of bed, got dressed, and then quietly tiptoed to the kitchen so she wouldn't wake up her kind hostess. To Antoinette's surprise, Sister Catherine was up and reading the morning paper. "Have a warm cup of coffee, my dear, and some homemade biscuits and jelly. They are scrumptious," the sister said, giving her guest a big smile and a wink. Antoinette gave the sister a good-morning hug and took her advice.

While she ate her breakfast, Antoinette couldn't help but revel in the coziness of Sister Catherine's home. Both the orphanage and the university felt different than this—more sterile. Although she hadn't changed all that much, Sister Catherine didn't look like a nun anymore. Antoinette's enjoyed her host's new farm girl appearance. Interrupting her thoughts, the sister asked, "What do you plan to do today?"

"Well, I have only one week before I start at the hospital. I planned on getting my license changed, opening a bank account, and getting a postal box. Then if there is any time left over, I want to just drive around to get a feel for the area. Would you like to come?" Antoinette replied.

The sister chuckled and said, "You know, Antoinette, I was old when you arrived at the orphanage and ancient by the time I left. These old bones are happy as heck to putz around here. Thank you, though." They both laughed.

Chapter 10

It had been two months since Antoinette officially started her employment as a physical therapist. She loved it. The staff was easy to work with, and the children were exceptional, with enormous amounts of determination to get better and complete trust in the routines she assigned them. It gave her an incredibly good feeling when one of her little patients got better and was able to go home. Then there were those few cases where not much improvement occurred. Antoinette worked harder with these children, thinking that her will alone could help them make one small step of progress. When it didn't happen, Antoinette was affected. Feelings of uselessness sometimes overwhelmed her. She was sensitive. Sister Catherine reminded her often that God asks nothing more of us than that we do our best.

"Have you found a place yet?" a coworker inquired at lunch one day.

"No. I've seen about ten different locations, but none seemed to work out. They are too expensive, in the wrong location, or just not fit to live in. Got any tips?"

"You know, now that you mention it, I just may have. Let me make a phone call." Antoinette's coworker dialed her cell phone. About ten minutes later, she was smiling as she hung up. "I found a place," she said. "And you, girlfriend, are just going to love it. It's not far from where you live now."

"Really? I've searched everywhere in my area and haven't found anything. Is it expensive?"

"Shouldn't be. And it just became available. The owners are friends of my parents. I think it is about $650 per month, but on five acres with all sorts of animals. It's what they call an in-laws' cottage."

"Oh my God, sounds perfect! When can we go see it?"

"You can go directly since you live down that way. They are expecting you. Here is their information. Just call them before you go." Antoinette thanked her friend and then finished up with lunch. She was interested in getting her work done as early as possible so she could go see the place that evening on her way home from work.

"I love it! When can I move in?" Antoinette said to Mr. Griffin.

"Well now, I've got to finish the painting and some do plumbing work in the bathroom. The place should be ready, I guess, at the beginning of the month. Would that be all right with you, ma'am?"

"Just perfect. And please, call me Antoinette. I'll give you a deposit now so you don't have to worry. And this gives me enough time to get my stuff together. I'm actually living pretty close to here at a friend's house. I think it's time I got my own place."

Mr. Griffin was his old curious self and kept Antoinette in conversation for about an hour until she stressed that she really had to go. *Friendly,* she thought, *but definitely not short on words.* Very excited, she couldn't wait to get home to tell Sister Catherine she had found a place to live.

"Oh, my dear, I'm sure you know what's best for you. But you know you don't have to go," Sister Catherine said sincerely.

"I know, Sister. And to tell you the truth, I've never felt more at home than I have living here with you. But I'm a big girl now and I've got to start making a home for myself. Do you understand? Besides, I'll be right around the corner. You won't even know that I've left."

"Ah, my dear, you are right about one thing: it's time you start making a home for yourself. Yes, I understand, but I'll miss you anyway. Let's get some supper."

The women ate, talking and laughing like they did every night—but this one seemed special.

Chapter 11

Luck or Fate?

Antoinette, having moved in to her new place, was absorbed in the tremendous sense of freedom she now felt. The place was perfect. For the first time, she could create her own world in her own home without outside influences. She sat at her kitchen table and started making a list of the things she needed to buy. Sister Catherine had been a tremendous help in getting her decent furnishings, but otherwise she needed everything. She decided that she would go to the store to pick up a few of the things on her list, including a pizza to bring home and bake.

Forty-five minutes later she was pulling into the driveway. The immense royal palms that lined the driveway made her feel like she was living in a place of grandeur. She slowed down for the extremely pregnant rat terrier that just stood in the middle of the drive and barked at her. Mrs. Griffin turned on the porch light, called for Candy to come to the house, and waved at her new renter. Candy begrudgingly obeyed. Humming a tune to herself, Antoinette unloaded some of the groceries. She popped the pizza in the oven before putting everything else away.

An hour later, the oven's timer reminded Antoinette to take out the pizza before it burned. She was on the phone with Sister Catherine, giving her the rundown of the day's events and updating her on the creature comforts she'd acquired in order to make her cottage feel like a home. After hanging up the phone, she paid attention to her dinner. It felt odd eating all by herself. *It's somewhat lonely,* she thought. *Does Sister Catherine feel this way? Maybe I shouldn't have moved?* "No, Antoinette," she spoke out loud to herself, "it's just something different that you have to get used to." After cleaning up her dinner mess, she took a shower and then retired for the night.

Exhausted, Antoinette lay in bed wide awake for half the night trying to decipher each and every country sound she heard. At almost 2:00 a.m., she finally drifted off to sleep.

In the following weeks, Antoinette quickly developed a routine, finally adjusting to her new home and independence. Though she wasn't too keen on being alone, she loved not having to account for anything to anyone, at least with respect to the makings of her house. She had sent cards to Ceci and Padre Alvaro but still had not heard from either one. She believed that Ceci must still be traveling, but couldn't understand why Padre Alvaro wouldn't call her back. Was he mad at her? Was he okay? Getting worried, she told Sister Catherine of her concerns. Her dear friend assured her that everything was fine and promised that she would contact the orphanage to verify the whereabouts of both Padre Alvaro and Ceci.

"Love means never having to say you're sorry," Antoinette said, repeating the words from the movie *Love Story* as she wiped a tear from the corner of her eye. She loved movies, particularly old ones and musicals, and had gotten into the routine of renting a film every Friday night. Life was perfect, she thought, except for the lonesome weekends. The movies helped her escape the loneliness she was feeling.

The movies she rented transported her to a time when chivalry was at its best and relationships were pure and innocent, a time when if two people truly loved each other, nothing else mattered. Sometimes while watching an exceptionally romantic and passionate flick, Antoinette would feel a sensation in her gut. She wanted a relationship but didn't know how to find that special person who would protect her and love her in a pure and romantic fashion. She had become aware of this desire at the university, but then she believed that the college boys were out for themselves. If that was the type of relationship available to her, she'd rather stay single.

In Miami, Antoinette was quickly learning from her friend's stories about the two sides of the passionate Latin. One side she was familiar with, the side that was dominating and controlling to the point of being abusive. It was the other side that intrigued her, the hot, melting passionate side, which was combined with a sense of familiar protection. But the men's abusive tendency kept her curiosity in check. No, she'd just as soon remain the spinster she was fast becoming.

At 8:00 p.m., Antoinette, a little bored, decided that since it was still early, she would take a walk outside. Just then the phone rang. It was Sister Catherine, with good news. She gave Antoinette Ceci's new address and the phone number to her home in Naples on the west coast of Florida. Sister Catherine, in keeping with her promise to the padre, delivered no news of Padre Alvaro's whereabouts, but she did say that he had left the church and moved away. Though concerned about the news about Padre Alvaro, Antoinette was happy that Ceci was located right here in Florida. She thanked the sister for her help.

Excited, Antoinette thought about whether she should call Ceci or write to her. *Surely*, she thought, *I should have received any correspondence by now, even if forwarded mail is slower than regular snail mail.* While tossing around the idea that she should call Ceci and let her know she lived in Florida too, she had a gut feeling indicating that she needed to see Ceci.

Quickly changing her mind about calling her friend, Antoinette went to her bedroom to pack her bags. She needed to see Ceci. Naples was just two hours away. She figured that she'd get there by 10:30 or 11:00, at which time she would get a hotel room. Then she'd surprise her friend in the morning. Antoinette, having a great deal to talk about, needed at least a day and a half to do it.

Leaving the Griffins a note about her whereabouts, and without a thought to whether or not Ceci would be there once she arrived, Antoinette left for Naples.

Halfway up the Tamiami Trail, Antoinette realized she was almost out of gas. Having passed a gas station a ways back, she thought about turning around. It was her first time traveling on this road; she hadn't realized how dark and desolate it would be. Barely able to drive under the torrential downpour, Antoinette decided to continue west to the next station, where she would gas up and wait for the rain subside a little. "Oh no, not now!" Her Nissan sputtered and stopped. She was out of gas. It was 10:00 p.m.

"Stupid, stupid girl," she scolded herself, pounding the steering wheel. After having a short-lived tantrum, Antoinette refocused and analyzed her options. Getting out of the car, she was forced back in by the pelting rain. With no phone, and no idea from where or when help would come, she turned on her flashers.

During the first hour, Antoinette threw three mini tantrums just because not a single car drove by. Further on into the night, two cars had driven by, but neither slowed to help—and she was afraid to go out and wave them down. No words could express her feelings about the lack of police patrol. And she saw were no signs for a call box. "Jesus, Mary, and St. Joseph," she said aloud, hoping that one of the individuals she'd summoned would hear her and come to her aid.

It was almost twelve o'clock now. Antoinette, stuck on a dark road in the middle of a storm, was afraid to fall asleep. In a fit of panic, she tried to crank her car again, knowing it wouldn't work. Beyond frustrated, she got out of the car, pounded on the hood, and began kicking the tires. She didn't see the other car pulling to the side of the road.

Chapter 12

Julian was pleased as he began driving the long stretch home from Naples. It was another successful evening for his exhibit at the gallery. *I've finally made it,* he thought to himself. After all those frustrating years of being an unknown, he would now obtain the reputation of being a professional in his field. Tonight had been big because he was offered the job of replicating original artwork for one very wealthy man's yacht. Apparently, the man found himself in a dilemma when Lloyd's of London refused to insure the originals that were on his small ship. An opportunist, Julian offered the solution of replicating the originals. The two had closed the deal with a handshake. The project would begin in August, so he had almost two months to prepare.

Very excited about his good fortune, Julian didn't mind the bad weather, which would add time to his drive home. The two-lane stretch along the Tamiami Trail was desolate at night and could be treacherous if one got stuck. Why the Miccosukee hadn't provided for better road service was beyond him, particularly given the mass fortune they were building with their casino. Passing the Immokalee sign, Julian directed his attention to driving. He turned the radio's volume up louder to keep him alert. The clock gleamed 12:05 a.m.

"That's the night that the lights went out in Georgia," sang Julian, wishing the torrential downpour would stop so he could speed up, at least to 35 mph. Suddenly he saw flashing lights on the opposite side of the road just ahead of him. "What the hell?" he whispered. Slowing down to check out the situation, he saw a young woman desperately trying to get her car to crank. *I need this now like I need a hole in my head,* he thought, he pulling off the road to offer his help. Seeing the woman get out of the car and bang the hood in apparent frustration, he whispered, "Christ," as the rain pelted him.

"What's wrong?" Julian asked, scaring the stranded woman half to death.

"I don't know. It just stopped. And I can't get it to start again," a startled Antoinette yelled above the weather.

"Come in my car so we can at least get out of the rain," Julian yelled back, surprised to see her backing away and shaking her head.

"No, thanks. Okay, mister? I don't ride with strangers. I'll get her fixed and running somehow. Thanks anyway," she shouted through the rain, backing toward the driver's-side door.

"Hey, lady, just trying to be helpful. That's all. I'm not sticking around here any longer than I have to. Don't you have a cell phone? someone to call?" He was yelling louder now since she had moved away from him. Embarrassed by her lack of preparedness and desperate, she shook her head no. "All right. I've got one. Let me see if I can get you some help. But I'm going back to my car to get out of the rain," Julian said, wondering why he was offering his assistance to someone who apparently didn't appreciate it. Antoinette jumped back into her car and locked the door. Her heart was pounding in her ears.

Julian was frustrated when he read the No Service message on his phone. "Murphy's Law," he whispered to himself as he got out of the car again. Noticing that the young woman was no longer standing outside, he saw her roll her window partially down. "Hey, lady, there is no cellular service out here. I wouldn't suggest you stay here by yourself at night in the middle of a storm on one of the most dangerous roads in south Florida," Julian opined through the partially rolled down window. "Now, as I see it, you can ride with me to the next service station or deal with things on your own."

Antoinette looked down, fear welling up inside her. Either way, she was up the creek, but at least she might have a chance of getting help at the next service station. Seeing her fear, Julian leaned against the car's partially opened window and reassuringly offered her a solution. "Listen, we can leave our licenses on the front seat of your car along with a note. Will that make you feel better about getting the hell out of the Everglades?" Antoinette conceded. Getting out of her vehicle, she slowly followed him to his car.

"Holy bejesus, what luck I have to be your knight in shining armor. Julian Mesas. It is my honor. And whom, may I ask, is the damsel I have just saved from the alligators?" Julian extended his hand in mock humor. Antoinette, smirking at his theatrics, extended her hand ever so gently.

"This distressed damsel would be Antoinette. Antoinette Gonzalez."

Wow, Julian thought to himself, *what a smile.* "Well, pleased to meet ya, Miss Damsel Antoinette. Let's get this here horse on down the road," Julian joked in his poorly spoken but funny John Wayne accent. Then he drove back on to the road. *Shit,* he thought to himself, looking at the clock, *it's almost 1:00 am.*

In the downpour, they headed east toward Miami. Julian stated that he had a friend who owned a station about five miles down the road, adding that he hoped it was open. Antoinette remembered it; that was the station she should have stopped at. On the radio, Magic 102.7 played the oldie but goodie "Spirit in the Sky." In his best theatrics, Julian emphasized the bass guitar.

Soon they pulled into the dark parking lot and just stared at the closed station.

"Murphy's Law strikes again," Julian whined. He turned toward Antoinette. "Okay, when all else fails, go to plan B, right?" he questioned.

"I'm really sorry, Julian," Antoinette said. Before she could finish her thought, she was stopped by a comical wave of Julian's hand.

"Honey, I do believe we have entered the twilight zone," he began. "Julian Mesas was an average man returning home after a long day's work. On his way, he spotted a distressed damsel beating her car, and offered to help her. Little did he know he was entering into the twilight zone," Julian said, perfectly mimicking Rod Serling's famous voice. Antoinette smiled but could not hide the look of worry on her face. *A babe in the woods, a scared doe,* he thought, wondering why he always found himself in these off-the-wall predicaments. "No problem, man. Smile. Be happy. Uncle Julian has got a plan." Julian was joking because he was tired—and now stressed out with a problem that wasn't his.

Noticing Antoinette's disappointment that the station was closed, he became more serious. "You live in Homestead. I live in the Gables. It's 1:30 am. I propose we make it to the end of the trail and book rooms at the Miccosukee Hotel, which is the halfway point. By the time we get there, it will be after two o'clock. After a good night's rest, everything will look better. What say you?" Julian said, laying out his plan to Antoinette. He watched her. She remained quiet for a moment. He could see she was trying to figure out another plan. Seeing none, she agreed to his idea. Julian smiled in relief, put his BMW into gear, and drove east.

Antoinette was quiet, wondering how he knew she lived in Homestead. Julian hummed the next tune, a Louie Armstrong song, and wondered why this beautiful woman was so uptight and obviously single.

The rain had subsided by the time they reached the casino hotel, an hour or so later. After a quick check-in, they said good night and went into separate rooms. Exhausted, Julian peeled off his suit and crawled into bed. *Christ, am I worn out* was his last thought. The clock radio read 2:45 a.m.

Antoinette held her head in her hands for a moment and squinted. It had been a frustrating and unusual night. She hadn't had one of these headaches in many years. It was almost three in the morning, but she took a shower because she felt disgusting. "Mother of God, it is almost time to wake up," she moaned as she crawled into the bed. Exhausted, she rapidly fell into a deep sleep.

Chapter 13

Julian woke up confused, not remembering where he was. As the sleep began to slip away, he recognized the décor of the room in the hotel he had stayed in a time or two before. Usually he was not alone, so he thought his singular presence this time to be quite odd. Still tired, he reshuffled his pillow and lay in bed thinking. Going over the events of the day before in his head, he chuckled upon remembering how nervous he had been on his drive out to yet another grand opening of his exhibit. For almost a decade he had produced art for exhibits. Although he had earned somewhat of a reputation and made a relatively decent living, he had not been presented with an opportunity that would give him the prominent recognition he aspired to—not until last night. He savored the moment when his client had agreed to his suggestion, with a handshake closing the deal.

His thoughts trailed off to his encounter with Antoinette. Thinking of all the creeps she could have run into, he believed that she was lucky he had been there to help her. The whole situation was odd. How could she be so unprepared? Damn the Miccosukee for not servicing the road better. Anyway, she was no concern of his, other than that he would like to see her get home safe. He had a few precious days left to really enjoy life before he began his big project—not, of course, that the project did not bring him total euphoria in and of itself. But a project like that required immense self-discipline that would deny him any long-term relationships with women. Any partner he would choose would never tolerate his absence. *God, but is she beautiful.* Scolding himself for even thinking this way, Julian jumped out of bed and showered.

Antoinette stretched like a lazy cat, indifferent to her surroundings. Silently she prayed to God the Father, God the Son, and Mother Mary for her safe arrival. *What was I thinking, making such a trip on my own at that hour at night?!* She had wanted to make a surprise visit to her dear friend Ceci. It was her first trip out west. She hadn't figured that there wouldn't be another gas station just around the corner. *Stupid, stupid girl,* she thought, squinting once she sensed the beginnings of another headache. "No way," she whispered, "I don't have time for this." She slipped out from under the covers to get dressed. Thoughts of Julian came to her as she readied herself. Julian had truly proven himself to be a knight in shining armor. She silently thanked God for that too.

Antoinette's reverie was broken by the ringing phone.

"Good morning, Miss Antoinette. This is your knight in shining armor calling," Julian said humorously on the other end of the line.

"Good morning, Sir Knight. How may I help you?" Antoinette volleyed back, smiling to herself. She enjoyed this stranger's bizarre sense of humor.

"Ah, an open-ended question. No, you don't want that answer. How about meeting me for breakfast downstairs before we hit the road?" Julian offered.

Antoinette agreed. As she hung up the phone, she wondered what he meant by, "No, you don't want that answer."

After gathering a few of her things, Antoinette almost ran into Julian as she exited her room. "Oh, excuse me for being such a klutz!" She fumbled through the embarrassing moment.

"It must be my magnetic personality. You know, I have that effect on women!" Julian chuckled as he watched her turn pink. Relishing the look of her face as she blushed, he politely extended his arm for her to grab, but she didn't take it. Awkwardly he gestured toward the elevator. Simultaneously they said, "I'm starved." Their laughter melted some of the ice as they walked down the hall.

Chapter 14

The elevator ride was quick and awkwardly silent. Antoinette was happy to arrive into a bustling lobby. Julian verbally guided her toward the restaurant, not daring to touch her. They waited to be seated. "Good morning, Julian!" a cheerful young hostess greeted, signaling for the pair to follow her.

"Suzanne, my dear, how are you doing? How are your children and hubby? I see you're keeping that fine shape of yours. Must be that they're keeping you busy! Let me introduce you to my new friend, Antoinette. Antoinette, meet Suzanne."

Antoinette picked up on the fact that Julian was friendly and definitely not at a loss for words. The women gave each other a polite hello before Antoinette and Julian were seated at their booth. Antoinette's gaze followed Suzanne. She wondered what her relationship was with Julian. Catching herself, she reminded herself that it was none of her business. But curiosity got the best of her. When she could no longer stand it, she asked Julian about Suzanne.

Julian understood women. Although he didn't really *know* the woman in front of him, she was, after all, a woman. In his experience, all women felt a hint of jealousy toward other women even if they denied it. Looking at the waitress,

Julian cautiously answered, "Suzanne? She used to work for me. I am a painter." He regarded Antoinette as a curious cat.

"Oh. I see," Antoinette replied, guessing that the young woman must have been his secretary.

In a friendly manner, Suzanne interrupted them by serving two fresh-brewed coffees and asking if they were ready to order.

Once Suzanne had walked away from the table, Julian said to Antoinette, "Now, my sweet, since we have had such an adventurous night together, could you tell me a little bit about yourself and how it was that you were traveling at that hour of the night alone?"

"Well, I just found out that a dear friend is living in Naples. I wanted to give her a surprise visit. I had never been west before and didn't think it would be such a terrible trip. I hate to admit it, but I think the only problem was that my car ran out of gas. I never thought that there would be so few service stations. I was stuck for more than two hours before you came. No one would stop, and I was afraid to wave down anyone for help. I can't even believe a police car didn't pass by. It's a good thing I didn't call Ceci before going or else she would be worried to death by now. Now I've got to figure out how I'm going to get to my car," a frustrated Antoinette answered.

"Hmm," Julian whispered. *She is definitely impulsive.* "Now that you mention it, I can call my friend who owns that station." Julian placed the call and spoke to his friend. He was smiling at Antoinette when he hung up. "No problem. They are going to tow your car to the station we went to last night. It'll be safe until you get there." He smiled. By the way, how do you plan on getting to your car?" Julian asked.

"I was just going to take a taxi. Boy, this is becoming expensive." Antoinette winced.

"No friends?"

"No, not really. I'm new in town. I haven't gotten myself established yet," Antoinette quietly explained.

They were interrupted by the waitress, who was ready to serve them two western omelet platters and juice. After waiting for Suzanne to finish refilling the coffee cups, Julian began to dig in. But he stopped as he saw Antoinette bow her head and say a quick prayer before eating. "You do this at breakfast?" Julian was somewhat embarrassed by her public display of praying.

"At each meal," a smiling Antoinette explained. Then she set to devouring the delicious breakfast. He was intrigued by this woman. Her impulsiveness and naivety were uncommon. "By the way, Julian, how did you know I lived in Homestead?" Antoinette asked after she took her last gulp of coffee.

"Ah, ancient Chinese secret, madam. ... Your license, remember?" Julian winked. Antoinette relaxed a bit, chuckling to herself for not having guessed the obvious.

Driving south on Krome Avenue, Julian conversed lightly with Antoinette to get a fix on where she lived, learning that she had just moved to south Florida about two months prior, taking up a position as a physical therapist for handicapped children at Baptist Hospital in Kendall. "Isn't that a bit of a drive for you?" Julian questioned. Working most of the time from the studio he had established in his house, he didn't care much for the overwhelming traffic.

South Florida was fast becoming the new "Big Apple"; everyone seemed to want a piece of paradise.

"Not so bad at all. I love the peace and solitude of being in the country. And the shift I work is not during the major rush hour," Antoinette said, pointing to the next street. "Make a left here onto 200th Street. I'm on 196th Street and 145th Avenue."

"But this really isn't Homestead. This isn't the address I saw on your license," Julian remarked.

"You're right. The address you saw belongs to Sister Catherine Rich, a retired nun I stayed with until I found this place," Antoinette explained. She then stated that she had been lucky to find the place she now called home.

"Not that it is any of my business, but you aren't a nun, are you?" Julian popped the question.

"No, just raised by them." Antoinette giggled, exposing a piece of her life to this stranger whose company she was beginning to enjoy. "Well, here we are." She pointed for him to turn into the driveway.

Julian stopped the car, impressed by the piece of property he was looking at. On the left there were horses roaming freely in a corral. The drive was lined by enormous royal palms, and to the right lay a mini mansion. "That's where you live?" Julian was incredulous.

Antoinette chuckled as she responded, "Sorry, but no. I live in the in-laws' apartment in the back. You can just leave me here, though. I'll walk in. I've bothered you enough."

Julian didn't want her to leave, he found her intriguing. "Tell you what. If you're ready by 5:00 p.m., I'm heading back out to Naples. You can catch a ride to your car and be on your way to see your friend," Julian said, scheming for another opportunity to meet her.

"You know, I don't know what to say. You've been so kind to me, Julian. I don't know how to thank you."

"My pleasure, ma'am. See you at 5:00 p.m. sharp!" Julian, not giving her an opportunity to change her mind, put the Beemer in reverse and quietly asked himself, "What am I doing?"

Chapter 15

Walking down the long drive, Antoinette was greeted by a small pack of rat terrier puppies with the mama dog herding them from behind. She loved animals and had helped name each one of the six little rascals. Antoinette couldn't help but laugh at the excitement with which the pups greeted her. She could be gone five minutes, five hours, or five days and the enthusiasm was the same. *Unconditional love is something I never had,* she thought, picking up her favorite, a runt named Chiquita.

The entourage followed as she headed toward her home at the end of the drive, behind the main house and across from the stables. Ducking into the stables, she sang a happy hello to Charlie, an older Appaloosa, and Magic, a young Quarter. She was a rider herself and was lucky to have found a place such as this that welcomed her helping hands in the care of the farm animals.

Antoinette took a deep breath and then slowly exhaled as she leaned against the cottage door. What an experience she had just had. She welcomed the warmth of her Dade County pine cottage. Scanning the living area, she noticed the clock on the wall. It was noon. Julian would return for her at 5:00

p.m. sharp—enough time to take a nap. She dropped her handbag to the floor and went into the bedroom. Peeling off the clothes she wore, Antoinette crawled into her unmade bed, snuggling into her down bedcovers and thinking that this place was the best spot in the whole world.

Lying there, she found that her thoughts led to Julian, a mysterious knight in shining armor. She liked him and thought him handsome. He was 5'9" or so, well-built, with the a body of a physical man. *Of course,* she thought, *a painter requires a strong back.* His black curly hair and Caribbean-blue eyes accented a perfect Roman nose. What intrigued her most was his bright smile lined with full lips.

Antoinette's thoughts then turned to the absence of intimate relationships in her life. At twenty-four, she had never been involved with a man. All her life, she'd tried to avoid the inevitable intimacy that dating required. She kept a tight control on her emotions, knowing that a meaningful relationship would require a level of trust she was not yet willing to extend. Julian excited her, though. She unconsciously began to get warm just before drifting off to sleep.

"Deny him. He is *el monstro*," the voice in her most violent dream began. Sweating and fighting with herself, Antoinette tried to escape the voice in her head, but she couldn't do it. She dreamt of being tied facedown on the bed with an ominous figure hovering over her, preparing her repentance. She cried in her sleep as she felt the snap of the whip across her bare bottom. "You are a naughty little girl and must be punished," the voice said before dealing out the next blow. Suddenly her dream changed in character. She felt someone untying her, gathering her, and kissing her along her temples, saying, "Don't worry, *chiquilla*, I will save you." Then she drifted back into the void.

Three hours later, Antoinette awoke in a sweat. She was exhausted. *Some power nap!* Dragging her achy body to the bathroom, she tried to remember her dream but couldn't, grasping only the bits and pieces that came to her that made no sense. "I'm going nuts for sure," she said aloud as she drew a cool bath. Music from the bathroom radio filled the room, pushing the extraordinary experience aside. "I've never been a sinner; I've never sinned. I've got a friend in Jesus," Antoinette sang to the tune of "Spirit in the Sky." Then she entered the soothing cool bath. The song reminded her of the previous night. Julian had sung it on their way to the closed gas station. She chuckled as she remembered him overemphasizing the bass guitar.

Antoinette's thoughts switched to the purpose at hand. Once she got her car gassed up, she'd be on her way to visit Ceci. Excited about her trip, she quickly finished her bath. Drying off in front of the mirror, she thought the bath had done her good.

Antoinette owed her life to this woman who had helped her through the loss of her parents. Though Antoinette had essentially forgotten what happened to her when she was young, Ceci often assured her that she and Padre Alvaro loved her very much. It was Ceci's encouragement that made her want to go to college, which is why she excelled in high school. Now, she wanted to thank Ceci personally and show her the fruits of her labor of love.

Antoinette pulled up the zipper of her jeans, put on a low-cut ruffled blouse, and looked into the mirror. She was pretty and she felt it. After dabbing on some perfume, she slipped on her shoes. Then she went to the kitchen to prepare a bologna sandwich. Wrapping the sandwich in a napkin, she picked up her purse and walked out the door. It was 4:30 p.m. She had time to check up on the Griffins and then be at the gate when Julian arrive.

The entourage of puppies trailed alongside her. She laughed as she tried to keep them out of the Griffins' house. The Griffins were always glad to see her, as not many people came by to check up on them. Antoinette gave a quick recap of her adventure, promised to be safe, and told them that she'd call them once she arrived at her friend's house. Mrs. Griffin remained in the doorway to see if she could sneak a peek at the stranger. Mr. Griffin hollered at her to keep her nose out of other people's business, adding that she needed to fix him something to eat instead of being so nosey. Barking her disagreement, Mrs. Griffin let the screen door slam behind her.

Just as Antoinette reached the end of the drive, she saw Julian's car. While closing the gate to the property, she noted the time: 5:00 p.m. sharp.

Chapter 16

Ceci awoke from a restless dream. She didn't dream very often, or at least she never remembered her dreams. This one was unusual; it was a dream about Antoinette. Ceci was shaken up by the fact that she'd never before dreamed of any of her patients. She looked over at her husband and decided to wake him; she was that disturbed. "Uh, what in the Lord's name? Ceci, what is wrong? Is there someone in the house?" Juan became fearful and alert.

"No, dear, nothing's wrong. I mean, nothing is wrong with me. But I think Antoinette needs our help. I had a dream about her."

"Oh, what was your dream? What makes you think she's in trouble?" Juan asked, sleepily lying on his side to face his new bride.

"Well, first, I never dream about my patients. Second, I saw her reaching out to me, but it wasn't her at all. It was Sadie, and she wasn't human. She was a doll. There was a man, but I couldn't see his face because he was in the shadows."

"My word, Ceci. Are you sure you didn't do drugs in your college years? Maybe you ate—"

"No, Juan, I've not had this experience before. I've never done drugs, and nothing I've eaten was out of the ordinary,"

Ceci said, cutting him off. "We've got to call her and see if she is okay," she insisted.

They both decided it was best just to get up early. Ceci put on a fresh pot of coffee. "You know, the last time I had contact with Antoinette was just before her graduation. I've been meaning to call her back, but with all the traveling we've been doing, I guess I didn't give it too much thought. I figured we'd be much more settled after our honeymoon." Juan spoke his feelings truthfully.

"I know what you mean. I should have called her for her graduation to let her know how proud we are of her, but I didn't do it. I wasn't sure if keeping such strong ties was best for either of us. Now I feel bad about it. What do you think she'll say about us tying the knot?" Ceci said.

"And … her not being invited?" Juan's forehead creased, showing his concern.

"If I know Sadie, I mean, Antoinette—I can't believe I just said that—she'll be a bit set off about the whole affair and about being kept in the dark. She'll get over it, but I think we need to call her today," Ceci said, answering herself.

"Okay. Now that we've got that out of the way, how about some lovin' for your husband?" Juan wrapped his arms around his bride and gave her a big smooch.

"Seriously, Juan, you are insatiable!"

"I've got quite a few years to make up for." He smiled and led her back to the bedroom.

"Honey, I'm going to run some errands," Juan informed Ceci with a quick peck on the forehead before leaving. Ceci sat at the kitchen table, her second cup of coffee getting cold. She was consumed with the meaning of the dream she'd had. She loved Antoinette but hadn't want to pursue the relationship too much after they both left the orphanage. Professional ethics mandated that she keep an emotional distance from her patients, but this rule was hard to uphold when it came to Antoinette. So during Antoinette's years at the university, Ceci slowly weaned herself from the relationship. At some point during that period, she had become emotionally involved with Juan, the former Padre Alvaro. "What a mess life can be sometimes," Ceci, who often spoke aloud to herself, said.

She knew her husband thought of Antoinette as the daughter he'd never had. As a matter of fact, she was surprised that he'd agreed to the wedding date and honeymoon that caused him to miss her graduation. She also knew that he had sent her a card for her graduation, but he didn't go into detail about what was actually happening in his life, namely, that he had left the church to marry Antoinette's former counselor. Sure, she and Juan had planned to tell Antoinette, but life was hectic with their own personal affairs. The time never really seemed right until now, Ceci supposed.

She understood why her husband had left the church. Antoinette was a large part of the equation. He hadn't found answers sufficient enough to resolve his moral dilemma. Were there exceptions to the Ten Commandments? He could not fault the girl for what she had done. He felt that he had been called to the priesthood for a special purpose. Helping Antoinette and others like her was a big part of that purpose. But after Antoinette, he could no longer handle the pent-up rage he felt from such abuses. Ceci also knew that deep down inside, Juan was a passionate man and very much dependent on strong family relationships. Leaving the church was a tough decision for him. Ceci knew he had his reasons for not telling Antoinette. She also knew that he wouldn't be ready until he thought Antoinette would understand. Another bit of information she had was that although Juan hadn't spoken to Antoinette for some time, he'd kept tabs on her through Sister Catherine. "Bless her soul," Ceci whispered before finishing her cold coffee.

Her thoughts turned to the dream. What did it mean that Sadie was in it? And why was she reaching out? Was Antoinette in danger? Who was the man in the shadows? The many questions caused Ceci to worry. She regretted not having kept a closer relationship with Antoinette. She got up and went to ready herself before Juan came back.

"Not a problem, Ceci. Please stop worrying. I left a message and told her we were in Naples. I said that we wanted to meet with her to catch up and take her out to dinner," Juan assured his wife. Ceci felt somewhat relieved, but she was not totally convinced that everything was all right with Antoinette. "Come on, let's get our things unpacked." Juan smiled and gave a telltale wink. Grabbing Ceci by the hand, he led her down the hall to their bedroom.

Chapter 17

The ride back to her car seemed quicker than the ride from the station to the hotel the night before had been. *Odd,* she thought, *how time can play tricks on you.* It had been a pleasant ride. Julian, as she had figured he would, talked a whole lot. She learned where he was from, how he ended up in Miami, that he was never married, and that he'd just landed a big contract in Naples and was going to close the deal over the weekend. He made sure that everything was okay with her car before leaving. She thanked him for all his help.

"Here it is," she whispered, reading the sign that pointed to Naples. It was just a little after 8:30 p.m. "Just a few more minutes and I'm there." Antoinette felt like she had ants in her pants as she got closer to her final destination. Turning into the development, she hoped that she was not too late. The map showed her that the next street over was Royal Palm Drive, Ceci's street. She drove up the street slowly, reading each of the house numbers before finally arriving at the place she was looking for. The lights were still on. Antoinette could barely contain herself. Slowly she pulled up into the driveway. *Why am I so nervous?* she thought just before ringing the doorbell.

A few moments later, the door opened. She found herself staring straight at Padre Alvaro. What a surprise! They both just looked at each other for a moment, surprised by one another, until Juan exclaimed, "Antoinette! I can't believe it's you! Come in. Please, come in. Ceci! Come quickly. I have a beautiful surprise for you!"

Ceci rushed out to the entryway and stopped in her tracks. She couldn't believe her eyes. "Oh my Lord! Oh, Antoinette! It is so good to see you!" She gave Antoinette a great big hug.

"I'm sorry if I disturbed you, but I just found out you were here, Ceci. I didn't know that Padre Alvaro was here too. I wanted to surprise you because it has been some time. I have so much to tell you. What a coincidence that you are here too, Padre! Or should I say Mr. Alvaro? I heard you left the church."

Juan coughed and motioned Antoinette to come into the living room. "Did you get my message?"

"Not at all, Padre. Excuse me. What should I call you? 'Mr. Alvaro' seems too formal. When did you leave it?"

"Just today, my dear. And yes, you're right. Please call me Juan. We have so much to talk about. What a coincidence. We just got back and called you, and now you're here."

"Got back from where?"

"Our honeymoon," Ceci answered.

"Your honeymoon? Wait a minute, you two got married?!" Antoinette was stunned, and it showed.

"I know, it still seems surreal to us too. We fell in love, Antoinette, sometime after you left for the university and I retired. Call it fate, I guess," Ceci nervously explained.

"I don't know what to say or feel. I think I'm happy, but this news comes as such a surprise. Why didn't you tell me? Why wasn't I invited to your wedding? Is that fair?" Antoinette's surprise was turning into anger. She felt excluded.

"I understand, Antoinette. Let us calm down some. You need to direct those questions to me and not Ceci," Juan said.

"I just don't understand."

"First of all, have you eaten?" Juan asked. Antoinette shook her head no. Juan motioned to Ceci to heat up some leftovers. "Everything is better when you're not hungry, so let's get some grub while we talk." She followed Juan into the dining room and waited for Ceci to appear. In between they engaged in some small talk. Juan could not help but notice what a beautiful and mature woman "his" little girl had become. Ceci appeared with a tray of lunch meats with all the makings for sandwiches, and a gallon of iced tea. Antoinette said her blessings and dug in.

"Okay, we have lots of things to talk about," Juan proceeded while Antoinette chewed her food. "Let me answer your first question, which, I believe, was why we didn't tell you about our courtship. Love is a funny thing, Antoinette. When we realized our true feelings, you were just starting your last year at the university. Our relationship quickly progressed, but we had not yet made our commitment to each other. I went through my own emotional crisis when I decided to leave the priesthood.

It was not easy. So I guess there was just so much going on so fast. And not being really certain of the outcome, I chose to not complicate your pretty little head with my issues. I didn't want it to affect your schooling. Your second question was why you weren't invited to the wedding. What can I say? I'm sorry, but since I hadn't explained to you anything about our relationship, I figured it was best to proceed with our plans and explain everything to you when we returned from our honeymoon. Our wedding was not a big wedding like you think. It was just us and a few witnesses. So please don't be angry, Antoinette. I love you, we love you, very much. I hope you can see how happy we both are."

Antoinette remained silent for a few moments. "I just felt excluded, that's all," she said, sulking.

"I know, dear, but here you are today. And we've so much to talk about. How about we start with you first? How was your graduation? How is your work? And how has, well, everything been since we last spoke?"

Antoinette's mood changed at Juan's suggestion. Becoming her usual bubbly self again, she went on to tell them all sorts of things, from her graduation to her living with Sister Catherine, from her new home to her employment, and lastly about the dramatic experience she had in getting to Naples. She and Ceci talked until 2:00 a.m. Juan had made a graceful exit about an hour earlier.

Showing Antoinette to her room, Ceci was grateful that Juan had brought in her bag before going to sleep. She gave her guest the rundown of where all the necessities were, and then she kissed her good night. Before leaving the room,

Ceci said, "Antoinette, you don't know how much it means to us that you are here. Sweet dreams."

Ceci closed the door and quietly went down the hall to her own room, where Juan was enjoying a good snore. Antoinette was in fact tired. She put on her nightshirt, skipping her normal routine of showering, and crawled into bed. In no time she was drifting off to sleep.

She was sweating, trying to reach out to the haunting doll that appeared. Having had the same dream again, Ceci awoke at 6:30 a.m. Juan was still sleeping, so she quietly lay there thinking about her dream. *Why was Sadie reaching out to me? Antoinette is not in any apparent danger.* She contemplated the dream for a full hour before Juan finally awoke.

"I'm starved. How about cooking us some breakfast?" Juan suggested.

Ceci didn't mention the dream to him. "How about you cook and I clean?" she offered.

"Deal." Juan jumped out of bed, threw on some clothes, and went to play chef in the kitchen. Ceci lingered in bed for some time.

Antoinette squirmed as she became involved with her dream. Julian was with her. They were on a hilltop somewhere overlooking the ocean. She could feel the breeze and taste the salty air. "Love means never having to say you're sorry," Julian spoke to her, holding her face in his hand. Then he kissed her. It was real. She could feel it. She was trying to hold onto it, but something was intruding into her dream. The smell of coffee and bacon broke through.

Antoinette opened her eyes. She lay there silent, thinking about her dream and how real it felt, until reality set in, crushing her moment of bliss. "Why would he want me? Wake up, Antoinette," she said, voicing her thoughts. Then she got out of bed.

Chapter 18

Juan, full of energy, greeted Antoinette with such exuberance that it made her smile. She gave him a hug and said, "Um, that smells good. I didn't know you could cook!"

"Ah, my little one, there are many things you do not know about me," he joked. After contemplating what he had just said, Antoinette agreed: there was a lot that she didn't know about him.

Knowing him as a priest was different from knowing him as just another man. "Okay. Tell me something that I don't know about you," she bantered.

"I bet you didn't know that at your age I was a gold-medal triathlete," he smugly replied, flipping the omelet.

"Really?" Ceci and Antoinette chorused.

Juan gave his wife an energetic hello and a kiss on the cheek. Antoinette felt funny watching the display of affection. Ceci brushed past him and gave Antoinette a good-morning hug. "What are you doing up so early?"

"Are you kidding? Who could sleep with these aromas!" Antoinette winked at Juan.

"Breakfast is ready, but it's self-serve, so come and get it!" Everyone grabbed a portion of the breakfast spread and then sat down to eat. Juan blessed the meal. The three of them dug in as if they hadn't eaten the night before.

"How about we take a walk on the beach and then go check out the art show at the Galleria? I heard there is a new exhibit. Antoinette, you do like art, don't you?" Juan said.

"Love it."

"Sounds like a plan. Let's go about 3:00 p.m. so it won't be so hot. You are staying another night, Antoinette?"

"Yes, but I have to leave early tomorrow. I'll have a long day ahead of me, as I have to work a double."

"No problem. You may have noticed we are early risers around here!"

"Good." She smiled and then excused herself to get dressed.

"Juan, how about you disappear for a while so we can have our girly-girl discussions?" Ceci smoothly asked her husband, hugging him from behind.

"I got it. I'm getting the boot?"

"Yup, but I'll make it up to you," she said, pinching him.

"Ooh, that hurts!"

"Big baby!" Ceci pushed him aside and began cleaning up the breakfast mess just as she promised while Juan got ready to "disappear" for a while. She needed some time alone with Antoinette to feel certain that she was okay. The dream she'd had twice bothered her. Never in her life had she dreamed the same dream two times.

"You know, Antoinette, we really had a great time traveling to Asia. We went to Singapore, Sumatra, and Sri Lanka. Oh, was it fabulous! You can't imagine how exotic this world is! We've got pictures. I want to show them to you, but first I want to give you some gifts we brought back for you. Juan picked two of them out." Ceci handed her guest three gifts, one from each country. From Singapore, Antoinette received a bronze statue replica of the Merlion, the country's official symbol of welcome—a beautiful design of a lion's head on a fish's body. Along with the statue was a sheet of paper giving the history of the object.

"Oh, Ceci, this is beautiful."

"We thought it would look nice in the entrance of your home since it is a symbol of welcome." She handed Antoinette a second gift, this one from Sumatra. It was a handcrafted wood plaque of one of the Sumatran mosques. The workmanship was spectacular.

"Odd that Juan would chose this gift. It is extraordinary."

"I thought so too and asked him about it. He simply answered that he thought it to be a beautiful piece of art and nothing more.

"Finally, we went to Sri Lanka. This last gift, I picked out."

Antoinette opened it, surprised by a brightly colored throw with a unique Asian pattern.

"Oh, how beautiful, Ceci. You two shouldn't have. I love all my gifts. Thank you." She got up from the couch and gave Ceci a great big hug.

"So, my dear, is there anyone special in your life?" Ceci asked, daring to broach the topic.

"No. I believe I'm destined to become an old spinster. Should've become a nun!" Antoinette joked.

"You know, Antoinette, a time comes for all of us when we must leave a place of comfort and walk down new paths that God has laid before us."

"Funny you should say that, Ceci. That's exactly what Sister Catherine told me when I first arrived. But God hasn't shown me any new paths when it comes to relationships." She explained to her friend that it was not that she didn't want a relationship; it was more that no one seemed to appeal to her at the university. And she didn't really know anyone in Miami. "I don't want just any man in my life, Ceci. He must be kind and loving and romantic. I want to feel safe and secure, knowing that I am protected. Otherwise, I'd just rather be alone and fend for myself."

"Sounds like you are looking for the 'perfect' man. But guess what? He doesn't exist!" Ceci chuckled at her own wit, lightening up the conversation.

"But isn't Juan the perfect man? Why else would you marry him?"

"No, my dear, he is not. Nor am I the perfect woman— and neither are you. That's not what a relationship is about. If you seek perfection, you will never find what you are looking for. It only exists in the movies. But if you enter into a relationship on the premise that neither one of you is perfect, then it is easier to focus on what's right and to overlook what's wrong, generally. A relationship takes work."

Antoinette didn't say anything, because she didn't quite agree with Ceci. She believed that perfection through self-discipline was the objective of life. *After all, Christ is perfect. Humankind is not. Doesn't the Bible encourage us to be as much like God as is humanly possible?*

Interrupting Antoinette's thoughts, Ceci asked, "What about the man you met on your way up here? What is his name? Julio?"

"Ceci, come on. Julian? I don't even know him."

Ceci, having planted her seed, left the conversation at that.

The two women heard a car door slam.

"That must be Juan. We'll look at the pictures later. Let's get ready to go to the beach."

"The beach was really nice. Thanks." Antoinette, feeling relaxed, was happy she had made the trip. They brushed off the sand from their feet and piled back into the car. After driving a bit, they stopped at a place called the Crepe House to enjoy the most scrumptious crepes in the world. Antoinette hadn't known that so much could be done with a crepe.

"It's a quarter to five now. How about we go check out the art exhibit?" Juan suggested. The women agreed. After a ten-minute ride, they parked way down the street from the Galleria. It was like a block party. A little section of town was cordoned off, with vendors and artists offering their foods and wares to all the people milling about. It looked fun. Antoinette was excited. She, Ceci, and Juan looked like just another family melting in with the crowd. They walked slowly, checking out all the expensive artisan crafts. At the end of the road was a big sign reading, "The Galleria Art Exhibit." They went in.

It took a moment or so for their eyes to adjust from the bright sunshine outside. The Galleria looked like a sophisticated place with special lighting. It had an ambience reminiscent of a museum. Following the signs that led to the beginning of the exhibit, Antoinette, Ceci, and Juan stopped to look at each piece of art. It was an interesting presentation focused on portraits, landscapes, and animals that looked like cave art.

Halfway through the exhibit, Antoinette froze when she heard a voice from behind her. "The damsel in distress! Antoinette, what a surprise!" It was Julian. Juan and Ceci turned around when they heard him call her by name. She just stood there not saying a word. She was caught off guard, paralyzed.

Ceci lightly pushed Antoinette forward. With a suggestive smile, she asked, "Antoinette, why don't you introduce us to your friend?"

"Oh, yes, forgive me. Ceci, Juan, this is Julian, the man who helped me when I was stuck on the road coming here."

"Julian," they chimed.

"It's our pleasure to meet you," Ceci said. "Thank you for helping Antoinette. She is very dear to us."

"Yes, I know. Do not mention it. It was my pleasure." He stood there smiling and staring straight at Antoinette to the point that she began to blush. Noticing the slight change in her color, Julian offered the three of them an individual tour of the rest of the exhibit.

"You work here?" Juan innocently asked.

"In a sense. Here, let me give you my card. I am the artist of this exhibit."

"Oh." Juan was impressed. Antoinette wanted to hide under a rock.

Ceci noted that Julian was very handsome, apparently well educated, and a man with obvious talent. She looked at Antoinette, who was hiding behind Juan as he gave them a detailed tour. He was not short on words. "Antoinette, what a coincidence we should meet again. If you are going to be in town tonight, may I take you out to dinner?"

"What a great idea," Ceci jumped in, gently elbowing Juan.

"Great. How about I pick you up at 8:00 p.m.? I'll be closing the exhibit shortly. That should give me enough time to change into something less formal."

"Perfect." Ceci agreed as if it were she who was the one being asked out. Juan, knowing that Antoinette was beside herself, couldn't help but smile at Ceci's impromptu behavior. *Women,* he thought. Understanding Ceci's intentions, Julian got the Alvaros's address and telephone number and promised to be there by eight.

"Now I apologize, but I must attend to the rest of the public." Julian excused himself and left with one great big smile.

Upon leaving the exhibit, Antoinette hissed, "How could you!" She was embarrassed by Ceci's bluntness.

"Why not, Antoinette? He seems like a nice man. Besides, we were planning on visiting you next weekend, so what we don't get time to catch up on this evening, we'll do then. What are you going to wear?"

"I don't want to go," Antoinette adamantly stated, leaving Juan and Ceci behind as she walked toward the car. She sulked the whole way home. Juan kept his mouth shut, thankful the ride was a short one.

At home, after receiving some insight into the situation from Ceci, Juan said, "Antoinette, come and talk to me." Still sulking, she slowly walked toward the kitchen table. She felt a lecture coming on. "Why don't you want to go out to dinner tonight? Julian seems like a good person."

"I'm so embarrassed, Juan! How can I go out with him now with what happened this afternoon? I feel like I wasn't even there!" Antoinette was angry. Ceci listened from the hall, not daring to interrupt.

"I see. And if Ceci hadn't encouraged you to go, would you have agreed?"

"I don't know. Probably not."

"Because you found him offensive when he helped you the other night? Did he hurt you in any way?"

She couldn't believe the way her hosts were behaving. "No."

"Then why are you so afraid, Antoinette?" Juan usually called a spade a spade.

"I don't know. I'm all twisted up. I don't know what to do or what to say to him. I don't know him well enough."

"I see."

"What do you see? You keep saying that," she said, getting argumentative with him.

"Nothing. It's just that you are missing out on one of the pleasures of life, that's all."

"What are you talking about?"

"Life is a journey, Antoinette, just one long road trip. We are born, we travel, and then we die so to speak, without going into our faith. And in this world, there are only two kinds of people, got that? Those who live in fear and those who do not. Needless to say, those who live in fear live a life of anxiety that locks them up so they miss out on the many pleasures of life. The other kind of people understand that there is only one journey. They know that the people meet along the way make and shape your trip. The more people you meet who do not fear living, the more depth there is to your life and the more opportunities exist. Shall I continue?"

Antoinette shook her head no.

"It is only a dinner, Antoinette, nothing more. It could be the worst dinner of your life or the best dinner you ever had. You won't know unless you go."

"All right, all right, I get the point," she said, getting up to go to her room and change.

"Antoinette." She turned to look at him. "I love you. Enjoy yourself tonight." Like a child, she made a funny face. Juan just laughed. Then he retired to his own room to let Ceci know everything was fine.

"Is she going to go?"

"Yes. You were pretty quick, Ceci."

"Think she'll hate me forever?"

"No, my dear, not if everything goes as you planned." Chuckling, he winked at her. "You are a sphinx." She smiled.

The doorbell rang. "I'll get her out the door. You stay here," Juan advised.

Juan checked his watch. It was 8:00 p.m. sharp. He liked punctuality in a person. Calling out to Antoinette, he opened the door for Julian, who stood there with two bouquets of flowers, one for Ceci. *What a romantic,* Juan thought, asking his guest to come in. The two men sat in the living room for a few minutes making small talk about where Julian planned to take Antoinette that evening. When Antoinette appeared, she was beautiful in a pink sundress and flowered sandals. Julian hadn't yet seen this feminine side of her and was entranced by her beauty. Neither said a word to the other until Juan coughed, breaking the ice. He pushed Antoinette toward the door. Julian followed. "You kids have a great dinner. And don't stay out all night!" He closed the door behind them, whispered a prayer, and made the sign of the cross. Then, determined to take advantage of the time alone, he went on the hunt for his wife.

Chapter 19

In a symbolic gesture, Julian held out his arm for Antoinette to grab, which she did this time. He walked her to the car. "You look beautiful tonight," he said as he opened the car door for her to get in. She took a deep breath while he went around to the driver's side. She was nervous; the palms of her hands were sweaty. "Okay, now for a fabulous night together. Do you like sushi?"

"I don't know. I've never had it."

"You'll love it. It's delicious," he said, shifting into gear. He turned the music up and began to sing the words to the song "Desperado" by the Eagles. Antoinette liked that song. She began to relax a little.

Antoinette looked at her date as inconspicuously as she could. He was handsome, and his cologne added to his aura of manly confidence. Remembering her dream, she smiled unconsciously, thinking that she'd die if he found out what she was thinking. Like a shockwave he asked, "Why are you smiling?" He'd caught her off guard again.

"Oh, nothing. I was just thinking about something Ceci said to me today," Antoinette lied.

"What? What made you smile? I want to know," he insisted, now smiling himself.

"Comes a time when we must leave our place of comfort and walk down new paths God has laid before us," she blurted. Then, realizing how stupid she must have sounded, she wished she could find that rock to crawl under.

Julian remained silent for a few moments. "You know, that is one of the most intense statements I've heard in a long time. I like it." He smiled at her and then shifted his attention to the road as they approached the restaurant. She couldn't help but notice his perfect white smile radiating against his tan-colored face.

Julian pulled into the Shu Shin Restaurant's valet parking area, received a ticket from the valet attendant, and walked over to assist Antoinette. Arm in arm, they walked into the restaurant.

The hostess received them and led them to a semisecluded room. They had to remove their shoes before entering. The room housed two mini tables and lots of pillows. *Oh God,* Antoinette thought, *we're going to sit on the floor!* The partitioning walls looked like they were made of wood and rice paper. The waitress, a petite Japanese woman, came and asked what they would be having to drink. "I'll have a cosmopolitan. And the lady?" Julian said, extending his hand toward Antoinette.

"White wine, please." The woman bowed ever so slightly as she left to get their drink order. Julian looked at Antoinette intensely. The energy emanating from him caused her to look up.

"Antoinette, thank you for coming this evening."

"Didn't have much of a choice, did I?" she jarred.

He laughed thinking of Ceci's manipulation. "No, she didn't give you much of a choice this afternoon, I have to admit. But when you got to their house, you did have a choice, so I want to thank you for coming with me tonight." His voice was warm and steady.

If he only knew, she thought. Just as she was going to change the subject, the waitress appeared with their drinks.

"You don't mind if I do the ordering, do you?"

"Not at all. I haven't a clue of what to order."

Julian ordered an appetizer to start. With a slight bow, the waitress left again.

"When you said you were a painter, I thought you were a commercial painter. I was surprised to discover you're an artist. I really enjoyed your exhibit. Why don't you tell people you are an artist?"

"Well, a lot of people act funny around artists, like we are aliens or something strange, so I just tell them I'm a painter to blend in. Actually"—Julian brought his head down and toward her, as if giving up a big secret—"if you must know the truth, I am an alien!" He couldn't help but laugh at Antoinette's expression. She got a chuckle at being reeled into his dumb drama. "Antoinette, tell me something. How come a beautiful woman like you isn't married?"

She almost choked on her wine. "That's a bit personal, Julian, don't you think?"

Caught off guard by her reaction, he thankfully was saved by the waitress bringing their hors d'oeuvres. *Touchy subject,* he thought. *Better back off.*

Antoinette, you did it again. Apologize, she mentally reprimanded herself. "I'm sorry, Julian. You just caught me off guard."

"I didn't mean—" Julian began.

"I know. I don't know why, Julian. Quite honestly, I've never found Mr. Right."

"I understand."

"You do?"

"Yes; I've never found Ms. Right either." She smiled. He offered a toast. "To us."

Chapter 20

"I ordered tuna tataki for our appetizer. It is actually one of my favorite dishes. And here they do it very well," Julian said, pointing at the dish after the waitress had left. "It is thinly sliced raw tuna marinated in a citrus soy sauce called ponzu. Have you ever had raw tuna before?" Julian asked, knowing Antoinette hadn't and enjoying the emotions evident in her face as she contemplated the dish. *First-time-sushi-eating emotions,* he mused.

"No," she quietly said with a fearful chuckle. She was having difficulty imagining herself eating raw fish, although she thought that the plate looked interesting.

"You'll love it! It actually doesn't taste like fish at all, more like meat. Have you ever used chopsticks before?"

"No, not really," Antoinette confessed, feeling totally incompetent.

"It's easy. Here, let me show you." Julian modeled the proper way to hold the wooden sticks, making them move like crab claws. Antoinette tried, fumbled, and tried again and again in exasperation. Politely, Julian reached over and grabbed her hand, repositioning the sticks and showing her how to use them. His hands were soft, and the intimacy of his touch made her feel warm. She pulled away and reenacted his steps. "Perfect. You'll be a sushi-eating expert in no time," he said, smiling at her. She smiled back, scooping up her first piece of raw flesh.

"Ooh, this is delicious!"

"I told you so." He chuckled and sipped the last of his drink. The quiet waitress presented herself again to explain that their meal was being prepared and to ask if they needed anything else. Julian ordered a bottle of Far Niente white wine while Antoinette took the opportunity to run through her prayer as quickly as she could. She finished as the waitress politely backed away to fulfill Julian's request.

This time Antoinette took charge of the conversation. "So, Julian, please tell me about this business of yours. How long have you been an artist?"

"All my life, really. As a child, I painted everything. It just was natural to me. So after high school, I went to Europe to study from the masters, so to speak. After that I came back to Miami and set up my own studio, where I still live and work now. I supported myself as a bartender by night and worked as an artist by day until such a time as I had a satisfactory collection to offer. I opened my work to the public through exhibitions like the one you saw today. Eventually, I was able to leave the odd jobs and do this full time. I also make portraits, mostly of models and old rich women!"

"Wow! It sounds so exciting, so glamorous. I love art, but I couldn't draw a chopstick to save my soul!"

"Well, like anything, of course, it can have its moments. But yeah, I am pretty fortunate. Now I've got my biggest client ever and I am so excited." Julian boasted like a peacock showing his prized fantail. Antoinette took another bite of the tuna, enjoying his youthful exuberance. The waitress returned with the wine and offered it for Julian's approval.

"So how come you haven't found Ms. Right yet? I imagine that you've met a lot of people during your travels through Europe and through your exhibitions."

"I do. I really don't know how to answer that question. Most women I meet are, let's say, charming—for lack of a better word—and beautiful. It's hard just to pick one. You know what I mean?" He chuckled.

Antoinette gave a nervous smile and thought, *A player. Stay way far away!* "I see."

Julian, watching her reaction, thought he might have been just a little too honest, a bad habit of his.

"Maybe I just haven't found that one true person, that soul mate. One day, maybe I will. And then, who knows, I'll probably settle down, have more kids than I can afford, etcetera, etcetera. Here's to becoming a married, fat, and bald family man!" he said, clinking his glass against hers. She couldn't help but laugh; he did have a great sense of humor.

The waitress reappeared with an artistic display of food. On a butcher block she brought a sculptured dragon. There was a side plate of sliced rice rolls filled with something that Antoinette couldn't quite make out. In a large bowl the waitress had brought a rice noodle salad. She bowed and left. "The famous dragon roll. Isn't it beautiful?" Antoinette agreed while Julian served her a bit from each of the plates. "The rice noodle salad is unique to this restaurant. I promise you, you'll make the trip back here just for this!" After he served himself, they both dug in.

"So how come you pray so much?" he asked between bites.

She studied him for a moment, trying to figure out if he was being serious or mocking her. "I'm grateful. Don't you believe in God?"

"In a universal intelligence, yes, but God, Buddha? Who knows? It's all the same."

"That would be like saying all painters are artists," she replied, calmly defending her faith.

"Maybe you're right. Maybe you're my guardian angel!"

"How do you like your meal?" he asked, now wanting to change the topic. Religion and politics were nothing but trouble. He should've known better.

"It is very good, surprisingly so. The rice noodle salad is outstanding," she said, allowing herself to be led away from the subject. "May I have more, please?" He smiled and served her a heaping spoonful, then offering more of the rolls, which she took.

"I like a woman with an appetite!"

"Good thing, 'cause I outeat most men!" He was amazed of this admission in light of her well-kept figure. *A nice model,* he thought, as he sipped more of his wine. Visions of her posed au natural with her long mane of curly red locks flowing over her shoulder came to him. Her skin was very white. He shifted the discomfort his thoughts had created.

They ate and conversed through the meal. Julian revealed his true storytelling abilities with various jokes and by making up stories of the people he targeted in the restaurant. "You should have been a comedian, Julian," Antoinette said, wiping a tear from the corner of her eye. She hadn't had such a good laugh in such a long time.

After they had finished their meal, Julian requested the check and settled the bill, refusing the money Antoinette offered.

"It would offend me greatly, Antoinette. You are my guest." The tone of his voice left no room for argument. "How about we go for a walk on the beach? The night is still young," he said, looking at his watch. It was 10:30 p.m. "I promise not to keep you out too late." Antoinette agreed.

Julian pulled his car into the public parking lot and noticed the moon was full and low—a champagne moon. He got out of the car and, like a gentleman, went to open Antoinette's door, but she had already gotten out of the car. "You are an independent, Ms. Antoinette. Next time, honor me, please, by letting me open the door for you."

So chivalry ain't dead yet, Antoinette thought. She was feeling heady from the wine she had drunk. They walked toward the water. Antoinette was mesmerized by the low-hanging moon, which looked as if it were just touching the deep black ocean.

"Oh, Julian, it is beautiful!" Antoinette spoke softly. Julian agreed, grabbing her hand to lead her down the beach. Antoinette, who had never been much of a drinker, laughed as she pulled her hand away, "Ah-ah-ah. A touch of the hand may lead to the touch of the heart!" Julian pulled her back by the shoulders, turning her around and kissing her on the lips passionately. He lost control. She was driving him mad, but did she taste sweet!

Stunned, Antoinette felt fire in her belly and began to shake. The emotion was too strong; she pulled away. In the next instant, she was so overcome by shame that she turned away from him and began walking back to the car, wiping the tears that had begun to roll down her cheeks. She had said nothing to Julian. He was overwhelmed by his passionate outburst. Confused by his own reaction, he just watched as she walked away. *What is she doing?* he thought, snapping out of his dreamlike state. Realizing what was happening, he ran after her. "Antoinette, I'm sorry. I didn't mean to offend you," he said to her back.

Shaking her head she whispered, "Julian, please just take me home." She was shaking. He could see it but didn't understand it. No woman had ever reacted that way to him before.

Quietly, Julian obeyed. "Damn," he whispered before getting into the car.

The ride home was awkward and silent. Julian's head was spinning; he didn't know what to do. Frustrated, he turned on the radio. "Isn't It Romantic?" by Rod Stewart, was playing over the jazz station. He began to sing the lyrics quietly. She definitely was not like other women. He wanted her more than ever, remembering the explosion of chemistry he felt when he kissed her. What was he thinking!

"I'm sorry, Antoinette."

She remained silent. Never having felt so good and so bad at the same time, she just wanted to get sick. *Don't you dare,* Antoinette thought, mentally trying to settle the urge to throw up.

What is wrong with me? she thought. Then she blurted out, "Julian, I think I'm gonna … Pull over, now!" Seeing her turn green, he pulled off the road; she was out the door before they came to a complete stop. Retching her guts out, she just wanted to die.

Julian tried to help her, but she wouldn't let him. Embarrassed beyond reason, she started to cry, whispering between sobs, "I'm sorry." Julian, aching all over, slowly approached her from behind, laying a hand on her shoulder.

"No problem, man. Remember, Uncle Julian is here to save his damsel from distress," he said in a caressing tone, hoping to lighten the mood some. She chuckled and began to recollect herself. "Are you all right?"

"Yeah, I think so. I'm sorry." He raised his hand to quiet her. Turning her toward him with his other hand, he gave her a large comforting hug. She melted. His scent and his strength made her freeze like a scared rabbit. He kissed the top of her head and then just held her for a moment; he could still feel her shaking.

"Chiquilla, let's take you home," he said, affectionately referring to her in the diminutive. She followed easily, as her head was now throbbing. Fifteen minutes later, Julian pulled up into the drive and noticed the lights were still on. *They are waiting up for her,* he thought. He thanked her for a wonderful evening, grabbed her hand, and kissed it in the most gentlemanly fashion before getting out of the car to walk her to the door.

"Julian, please forgive me. I don't feel so well right now. I must go. Thank you for a wonderful dinner," she said. Turning, she went into Ceci and Juan's house. Quietly closing the door behind her, she turned off the lights and then walked toward her room. She was thankful that Ceci and Juan had actually gone to bed, which was all she herself wanted to do after taking a shower. She felt exhausted, emotionally drained, and angry at herself.

The cool water had made her feel better. She crawled into bed. She needed to be on the road by six o'clock, and it was already coming up on twelve thirty. After setting her alarm, she turned off the light and rolled over on her belly, hugging her pillow. She just lay there thinking about Julian and their kiss. Wanting to melt, she could still smell him. *Why didn't I give in?* was her last thought before succumbing to sleep.

Julian climbed into his BMW and slowly drove away. "What a strange night," he whispered. She had left him in a mess—first happy, then passionate, and then worried and confused. She had caught his attention, yet she apparently wanted nothing more of him than his friendship. Most women, he thought, would have succumbed right there on the beach, and then hound him for a commitment he was not willing to give. He thought about their kiss and became angry with Antoinette and himself. Needing a friend right now, he thought of Suzanne back in Miami. *Too bad she got married,* he thought, beginning to wonder if he hadn't missed an opportunity with her. "Give it up, Julian. You don't need this anyway," he said, shifting gears as he pulled into the hotel parking lot.

Chapter 21

Julian set the alarm for 8:30 a.m., methodically removed his clothes, and crawled into bed. He lay there restless, thinking about Antoinette and wishing he'd just fall asleep. She made him feel lonely and he didn't like it. He thought about his age, approaching forty, and wondered if it wasn't time to settle down a bit. Tiredness slowly overcame him. He closed his eyes with a vision of kissing this strange and beautiful woman. Minutes later his dream began.

She was a beautiful woman, the perfect model. Her long red hair with big natural curls draped over her shoulders, framing her oval face and flowing over her porcelain skin down to the small of her back, like a royal robe. She sat there in a tall, straight pose, one that only a model au natural could endure, not moving. He painted her ever so painstakingly, capturing every detail. With her legs crossed and her delicate hands folded over her most private part, she held a regal position that emphasized her flat belly, perfect small and upright breasts, and long neck. Quietly, he outlined her face on the canvas. His soft strokes caught the full lips, the small Mediterranean nose. Stopping momentarily as he reached her piercing emerald green eyes, he felt a shiver go up his spine. Suddenly her face became an angry contortion. She rose, seeming larger than life, and went toward him. Fear welled up inside him. He turned to run, but it was too late.

Julian awoke in a sweat, his heart beating madly. "My God" was all he could whisper. He hadn't had a nightmare like in a very long time. Looking at the alarm clock, he saw that the time was 3:00 a.m. Groaning, he flip-flopped in the bed, repositioning himself. Closing his eyes, he could still see the fire in her eyes. Frustrated, he reached for the light. Picking up the remote, he turned on the TV.

Ceci, hearing a scream, bolted upright from her sleeping position. "Juan, something is wrong with Antoinette," she said, turning on the light to find her robe. By the time Juan became coherent, he noticed his wife was rushing out the bedroom door.

Ceci tapped very gently on Antoinette's door and pushed it open, not waiting for her to respond. The room was dark. A faint shaft of light from the hallway allowed Ceci to see that Antoinette was having a nightmare. She was kicking and trying to scream, but her voice was muffled. "Antoinette," Ceci spoke softly.

"Go to hell!" a deep voice shouted. Antoinette was still dreaming and did not recognize Ceci's presence. Ceci's blood curdled as she recognized the old familiar voice— Sadie's voice.

Juan fumbled in and saw Antoinette in an agonizing state of commotion. "Antoinette, wake up." He turned on the light to help wake her.

"She's not here." Juan froze at the words that did not seem to come from his little girl. He looked at Ceci, frightened by what he was beginning to understand was happening. His wife was still and motioned for him to be silent. She was not sure if Sadie appeared only as part of Antoinette's dream or if the alter was in fact reappearing.

"Sadie?" Ceci quietly inquired.

"Yes."

"Why are you here?"

"To protect Antoinette."

"From what?"

Silence.

"Sadie, where is Antoinette?"

Silence.

Ceci motioned for Juan to try.

"Antoinette?" No response. "Sadie?"

"Come closer and I'll kill you!" Sadie threatened Juan in a steady low voice. They could see Antoinette go limp, but her eyes continued to flutter behind her lids, indicating she was still in a dream state. Ceci motioned to Juan to follow her out of the room quietly.

"Something happened tonight," Ceci spoke pensively once they were in their bedroom. "She's afraid."

"I'll kill the bastard if he hurt her," Juan said, pounding his fist into his hand.

Ceci knew better. "Juan, it may not be that at all." Remembering her dream, she began to realize that she had been sent a premonition. Juan listened to his wife explain the dream she had. Then she mentioned that she'd the same dream one other time since the night before Antoinette arrived. Ceci believed that God had sent her a message to help Antoinette.

"In all my years of dedicated service, the Lord has never spoken to me in such a way," Juan voiced his thoughts. Realizing that he probably shouldn't have, he turned and asked Ceci, "What do we do now?" Her brain was spinning and she was somewhat taken aback by her husband's words, which indicated that he didn't believe her.

"Nothing. Right now we can do nothing except keep a watchful eye on her tonight. If I'm right, in the morning she won't even realize what happened. That will be a problem in and of itself. I think I should go stay with Sister Catherine," Ceci said. Then she made an attempt to sleep for the few moments of nighttime that remained. Juan drifted to sleep with his thoughts bringing him back to the day when he'd first helped Antoinette. Ceci just lay there until she decided to get up and prepare a travel bag.

Antoinette wrestled herself in her dream. In a flash she was feeling Julian's passionate kiss, and in the next instant she was living a violent rape. In the background she heard the old familiar voice, Sadie's voice, humming her to sleep as she had done so many times before when she was a little girl.

Chapter 22

Antoinette awoke exhausted. Hitting the snooze button, she was taunted by the odor of bacon seeping through her door. Music was playing. *My God,* she thought, *they have gone completely nuts.* Looking at the clock and seeing it was only 6:15 a.m., she begrudgingly pulled herself out of bed. Gathering her things to get dressed, she began to ready herself for the long drive to work.

"I think you guys are a little bit nuts! What are you doing up this early in the morning? Aren't you supposed to be retired? And fixing breakfast and playing music no less!" Juan and Ceci smiled at each other and then at Antoinette, who apparently remembered nothing of her dream. The newlyweds laid on the breakfast spread, and then the three of them gathered at the table, prayed, and jumped right into their morning meal.

"I'll miss this." Antoinette held her stomach and laughed. "But I better get going or I won't have a job!" Her hosts agreed. Juan gathered her luggage. Ceci held her hand in a motherly fashion and assured her that they would be down for a visit soon. Antoinette felt loved pulling out of the driveway and heading toward I-75. Looking at the clock, she determined that she'd arrive before 10:00 a.m., a little earlier than the start of her shift. Ceci grabbed her bags as she watched Antoinette drive away.

"Sure you want to do this?" Juan questioned.

"I must. I love you. I'll call when I get there and let you know how things are going. Think you can make a weekend trip?"

"Let's see. Be safe." Juan hugged his wife and helped her with her bags.

Julian awoke groggy. He could still feel the fear that had awakened him from his dream. He looked at the clock and saw it was 8:30 a.m. He was already a half hour behind schedule. Forcing himself up, he shook off the ill feeling that lingered from the night before and then jumped into the shower. *Amazing what water can do for the human body,* he thought. He let the hot water pound his back. He was achy but slowly became energized. He finished his shower humming a tune. "Isn't this love?" he sang, stopping for a moment to contemplate the lyrics to the song. After getting out of the shower, he dried his hair and made a move to get dressed, stopping for a moment to take a look in the mirror. He still had a great shape, but he wasn't getting any younger. Noting the few white hairs that crowned his head, Julian was having an age crisis and he knew it. Frustrated, he left the bathroom and got dressed.

Julian packed his bags and opened his agenda book to Monday. Though he had no appointments pending, he needed to check up on the packers that were moving his exhibition back to his Coral Gables studio. He had one more local exhibit before he left the circuit and became a solo artist for his new client. He needed time to study the paintings he would replicate and to make sure he had the appropriate supplies. Checking his watch, he saw it was already 9:45 a.m. He needed to go.

The notes stuffed in his agenda book flipped as he was closing it. He caught a glimpse of one particular note of interest. It was Antoinette's home number and address. Studying the note, he let his thoughts drift back to the beach when he kissed her. *Damn,* he thought. Remembering the explosion of passion that welled within him by just simply kissing her made him want her. He could just imagine what making love to her would be like. Although that night hadn't ended like he had hoped, Julian silently rationalized that it seemed to make him want her more. She wasn't easy like all the other women he knew. His imagination began to run wild with the exuberance of a teenage boy falling in love for the first time. He schemed for another chance to be with Antoinette. "She's working today," he spoke out loud. Then he gathered his belongings and went to his car. He had a plan to visit Marci, the local florist.

Upon arriving at the florist shop and walking up to the counter, he asked, "Marci, can you make it happen?"

"Julian, I've never seen you like this before." Marci cajoled her client and longtime friend. Julian, able to feel that he was blushing, coughed to gain control of himself.

"Seriously, Marci, it has to be the freshest, most exotic arrangement. Do you think they'll find her at the hospital? All I know is that she's a physical therapist for children."

Giving her friend a look that read, "Why would you ever doubt me?", Marci asked, "And the note shall read?"

"'Antoinette, call me. —Julian.' And add my number."

"That's it?"

"Yes."

"What a romantic." Marci emphasized her sarcasm with a roll of her eyes.

"Marci, you are a doll. I love you!" Julian smiled, blew her a kiss, and walked out the door. He was ready to get back to work.

Chapter 23

By 3:30 p.m. Julian had finished overseeing the packing up of the exhibition and had settled his account with the gallery owner. The split was fair, giving him enough money to pay some bills. More important than that, though, was the fact that he had won a prize client. After grabbing a bite to eat, he was on the road again. It was almost 5:00 p.m.

When he reached the Tamiami Trail, Julian realized that Antoinette had not called him. He called Marci. She assured her lovestruck friend that the flowers had been delivered and received at 2:45 p.m. He thanked her, feeling somewhat disappointed that Antoinette apparently hadn't felt any urgency to call him. He was not used to this.

Julian turned up the music and sang along with the radio, thinking about his first encounter with Antoinette and the events that followed. Revisiting last night's dream, he was certain that the woman in his nightmare was Antoinette. What did it mean? Was it a reflection of the events that already took place, or was it an omen? His thoughts turned to her shaking after they had kissed. *No omen,* he thought, *just a stupid dream.* He imagined how he had envisioned her in his dream and became uncomfortable just thinking about it. It had been a while since he'd had a decent roll in the hay. Antoinette was lighting up all the fires. He was in pain.

Antoinette received the beautiful arrangement at work. The girls cooed over the bouquet and tried to pry into her business. "So who is Julian? A true romantic! Why didn't you let us know you were dating someone, Antoinette?" one of them asked. As much as Antoinette tried to deny any relationship, her coworkers didn't believe her.

What should I do? She pondered her options as her fingers slowly rubbed the card. She began thinking of him, recalling their kiss and the overwhelming sensation it had produced. Just as her thoughts turned to her reaction, she was wakened from her reverie. Her next patient had arrived.

It was 11:00 p.m. Antoinette's double shift had ended. Gathering her things from her locker, she saw the card that had come with the flowers fall out of her pocket. Frowning, she checked her watch. It was already 11:15 p.m., much too late to call. Switching out her shoes, she grabbed her purse and left for home. It had been a long day. She decided to call Julian in the morning.

Ceci had arrived early at Sister Catherine's house. The two had spent the whole day catching up on events that had transpired since they'd both left the orphanage. Sister Catherine listened intently to Ceci's explanation of Antoinette's reaction to having a date with the artist. Although Ceci wasn't sure how Antoinette would react to her impromptu visit, she explained to her friend that her instinct told her she must come to be near Antoinette.

"Why don't you just tell her the truth?" questioned Sister Catherine after a moment of contemplative silence.

"What, that I am having strange dreams involving a doll representing her past personality and the man who has taken an interest in her? Or the part where she was dreaming and Sadie spoke to Juan and me? I don't think it'll be that easy, Sister."

"Comes a time when we must leave our place of comfort and walk down new paths God has laid before us," Sister Catherine reminded her friend.

"What is that supposed to mean?"

"Well, as I see it, you believe you were given a sign by God that involves three people: Antoinette, this man named Julian, and Antoinette's second personality, Sadie, represented by the doll. Before you 'analyze' Antoinette's mental stability, maybe you should analyze your dream. If it truly is a sign from God, then the answer will be there. Then you can know how to help our young friend."

"Maybe you should have been a psychiatrist, Sister," Ceci joked. They both had a good chuckle before agreeing it was a good time to call it a day. Sister Catherine led Ceci to the guest bedroom.

Ceci lay in bed thinking about Catherine's advice and the answer she was seeking. She wasn't finding any answers, but she felt an urgency to help Antoinette all the same. Sadie had said she was there to protect Antoinette. From what, though? Ceci believed the man in the shadows to be Julian, but she couldn't be sure. She just sensed it was him. Why was he in the shadows? Did he have some dark past that Sadie felt she needed to protect Antoinette from? Many questions kept running through Ceci's mind, but there were no answers. Ceci silently prayed for an answer to come to her in the night. Then she let herself drift off into the sleep she sorely needed.

When Julian arrived home, it was almost 9:00 p.m. She hadn't called. Why? He wanted to hear from her, as he was feeling lonely. Tired, he unpacked his things and crawled into bed with a book. He read superficially as thoughts of Antoinette entered his brain. Why hadn't she called? Frustrated, he turned out the light and lay in bed until sleep overcame him.

The dream began sometime around 1:30 a.m. He tossed and turned, groaning. She got up and was bigger than life. Julian awoke in a sweat and knew he wouldn't be able to get back to sleep. He needed to see Antoinette. For some reason he knew that this is what he needed to do to make his nightmare go away. Giving up on the idea of sleep, he turned on the TV.

Arriving home, Antoinette dropped her bag by the door and went to her bedroom. It had been a long day. All at once she felt exhausted. Shedding her work clothes, she jumped into the shower. After quickly drying off with a towel, she donned her nightie and jumped into the comfort of her bed, her favorite place in the world at that very moment. In no time at all she was fast asleep.

Chapter 24

The break of dawn brought Antoinette back into the nightmare she had dreamt the night before at Ceci's. Again, she wrestled herself in her dream and flashed between feeling Julian's passionate kiss and living a violent rape. In the background she heard the old familiar voice, Sadie's voice, humming to her. The voice sounded so real that Antoinette awoke with a start and looked around like a frightened child. She was met with silence. Relaxing back onto her fluffy pillow, she read the clock. It was 5:45 in the morning. "Oh God," she groaned, hoping she would fall back to sleep. She closed her eyes and went over her dream. What was that voice? It sounded so familiar. Then she thought about Julian, and how sweet the passionate kiss was until her dream turned into a scene of rape. She was being raped by Julian! "You're mad, Antoinette," she said to herself. Seeing the futility of trying to go back to sleep, she got up and prepared her coffee.

Actually, dawn was Antoinette's favorite time of the day. Grabbing her fresh-brewed coffee, she strolled outside to greet the morning. With an awesome view of the sunrise from her property, she reveled in the spectacular display of colors. As she walked past the Griffins' house, she thought about Julian and her dream. She knew he would never do her any harm, but she was afraid of the relationship nonetheless.

She was afraid of the intimacy and her own vulnerability. What if love wasn't like in the movies? Hadn't Ceci been adamant about that? No, there were no guarantees, so she had better stay away from the possibility of being hurt.

She remembered the years she had spent at the orphanage. One day she had felt like she awakened from a dream, a really bad one she knew of but couldn't totally remember. Ceci and Juan had always been there for her, like the parents she never knew. She was lucky, though. Vaguely remembering her father, she thought that God was merciful enough to send her Ceci and Juan. In a way, she had been given a second chance at having a family. Ironic, she thought, that Ceci and Padre Alvaro had ended up marrying each other. She knew she was like the daughter they never had. *A family.* She sighed. Antoinette's happiness had grown the moment she sensed she belonged to a family. She wanted a family of her own and didn't want to become the spinster she was fast becoming. "Comes a time when we must leave our place of comfort and walk down new paths God has laid before us." Antoinette whispered the words as she approached her cottage. Sister Catherine and Ceci had both said that to her. Wasn't that exactly what Juan had done when he left the church? Antoinette just wished she could step outside her comfort zone.

She decided against calling Julian that morning. If he was truly serious, he'd reach out to her again. And if he was not, she was okay with that. After all, she was independent and quite happy on her own.

Antoinette decided that she would pay Sister Catherine a visit before going to work. She'd be working the night shift for most of the rest of the week but thankfully no more doubles.

Julian awoke in a sour mood. All night he had drifted in and out of sleep, trying to avoid the nightmare. Sleeping with the TV on always left him feeling unrested. He was mad at Antoinette, and at himself for that matter. She should have called. There was no reason for her not to, particularly after receiving the beautiful floral arrangement. He was mad at himself for letting his guard down and becoming emotional. That was out of character for him, but hadn't seemed able to help himself. He felt obsessed, battling himself throughout the morning. *Should I call or wait?* was the internal conflict he wrestled with.

"Why should I call her? I made the first move." Playing his own game of devil's advocate, Julian responded, "Because you want her and she isn't playing by your rules! Ah, to hell with you!" Julian sighed as he picked up the phone and dialed. Disappointed that Antoinette didn't answer and second-guessing himself, he hung up without leaving a message. He was not happy.

Antoinette grabbed the flower arrangement and her bag and was out the door. She was on her way to Sister Catherine's and didn't hear the phone ringing over the pack of puppies that greeted her enthusiastically. She laughed and shooed them away, trying to get her car door closed. Slowly she pulled out of the drive, chuckling again as she looked into the rearview mirror and saw the pack running behind her. Mrs. Griffin appeared on the porch, waving and trying to distract the dogs. A few minutes later, Antoinette pulled up into Sister Catherine's driveway and noticed she had a visitor.

Chapter 25

Ceci awoke with a start. The answer had just hit her like a ton of bricks: Sadie was protecting Antoinette from having a relationship with the man in the shadows, and he was any man, not necessarily Julian. No one was trying to hurt her; just the opposite. In Ceci's dream, Sadie, the doll, held out her hands as if asking for help. This part stumped Ceci for a few moments until another flash of clarity came upon her. Sadie was asking for help because Antoinette wanted to have a relationship! "And that is why she appeared in Antoinette's dream! I've got to see her now, Juan." Ceci explained her understanding of her dream to her husband over the phone. "You see, Juan, God does answer us if we listen." Juan remained silent.

"So how long are you going to be?" he asked, changing the subject.

"I'm not sure. Maybe 'til the weekend. How about coming down on Friday? Are you all right?"

"Yeah. We'll see about the weekend."

"All right, dear. I'm just getting up now, so I'll call you later. I love you." Ceci sensed that Juan was irritated. Was it something she'd said? Shrugging at her own question, Ceci readied herself to greet her hostess.

Ceci was smiling to herself when she turned the corner, only to find Sister Catherine visiting with Antoinette. She stopped dead in her tracks. "Antoinette, hi. What are you doing here?"

Incredulous, Antoinette responded, "Hi, Ceci. What are *you* doing here? I live right around the corner, remember?"

Hurrying to hug Antoinette, who still looked astonished, Ceci lied. "Didn't I tell you that I had some business to take care of in Miami?" Antoinette nodded her lack of acknowledgement. "Oh, sure you remember. Remember I said we would be in town on the weekend to see you?" This Antoinette remembered; she slowly nodded her agreement.

"Is Juan here?"

"No. He had some things to take care of back home, but he'll be down on the weekend. I decided just to stay here with Sister Catherine knowing you had a lot of work scheduled this week. I figured that we'd see each other on the weekend." Antoinette again nodded her agreement. Then she looked at Sister Catherine, who was pretending to read the paper and silently was praying to God to have mercy on Ceci for her white lie. "What a gorgeous flower arrangement. Sister Catherine, did you just receive them?" Ceci asked, changing the subject. She touched the flowers that Antoinette had brought her friend.

"Oh, yes, Antoinette just brought them in. She received them yesterday from a friend and thought they would be better taken care of here."

"Really? Antoinette, who sent you the flowers?" Curiosity overwhelmed Ceci.

"Believe it or not, Julian."

"How romantic. But really, Antoinette, you say it as if he is the Grim Reaper himself!"

"Might as well be. Anyway, how about staying with me tonight? I have the day off tomorrow."

"I'd love to. Did you call him?"

"Who?"

"Julian, silly. To thank him."

"No, not yet. Well, I really have to go and get ready for work. I'll call before leaving for work. Love you both." Antoinette kissed both women and was out the door, happy to avoid the subject of Julian all together. Ceci shook her head after Antoinette had shut the front door. Then she turned to tell Sister Catherine about her exciting revelation.

Julian spent the entire morning trying to study the paintings he was going to replicate. Many people didn't realize the extent of study that went into a project like this. Checking his watch, he sighed about his lack of concentration. She hadn't called him, and he couldn't reach her at home. Needing a break from thinking about Antoinette, he decided he'd go out that night. Even though it was only Tuesday, he could use a good drunk with his friends. In a defiant manner, he turned off his cell phone.

Antoinette finished getting ready for work and sat down to pay some bills before she left. Fumbling through her purse for her checkbook, she came across the note Julian had sent with the flowers. She should call him, at least to thank him. But what else would she say? She hated being put in this type of predicament. She thought again about Sister Catherine's and Ceci's advice. Setting her papers aside, she grabbed the phone and began to dial.

After several rings, Antoinette heard Julian's voice. Her heart beat rapidly before she realized it was his voice mail. She choked and hung up before leaving a message. "You fool, at least you could have said thank you," she reprimanded herself, deciding she would try again later.

Looking at the phone, she decided to call Ceci to ask her come over before she had to leave for work. At least Ceci would have the key and gate access to come and go as she pleased while Antoinette was working.

A half hour later, Ceci greeted her at her new home. "Oh, how charming!"

"You like it?"

"Beautiful, Antoinette. You have a beautiful place." Antoinette was proud of her little cottage, and it showed. After giving Ceci a quick rundown of where things were, she handed her a gate opener.

"Make yourself at home. The Griffins are friendly, and the pack of pups will love you to death! I'll be home by 11:30 tonight. Then we'll have the whole day tomorrow. I'll call from work. You remember how to get back to Sister Catherine's?"

"Yes, dear, go on. I'll be just fine. Don't worry."

Antoinette gave Ceci a big hug and then left for work.

Chapter 26

By 9:00 p.m., Julian was smashed. His longtime buddy Tommy had agreed to meet him at their favorite hangout, Mr. Moe's, in the Grove. "She's evil," Julian slurred. He had recounted his dream at least three times to his friend. Tommy couldn't believe his eyes and ears. First of all, Julian never got drunk, and second, he never fell in love.

"Julian, she's not evil. You're in love, you fool!"

"Love? Phewy, what's that? No, man, she's evil. Did I tell you about my dream?"

"Oh yeah. Please, not again. Just sounds like you're afraid of a commitment."

"Hey, good buddy, listen to your friend. He's right: you're afraid of a commitment," the bartender said, unable to help overhearing their conversation.

"How do you know?" Julian seemed to have a moment of clarity.

"'Cause you dream of her being something you fear. You fear her 'cause it means you'd have to commit." Julian swallowed the last of his drink and ordered another.

"Maybe we should go, Julian," Tommy urged his friend, seeing that he was drunk.

"Why?! Can't sleep. She keeps showing up in my dream. She's evil, I tell ya," Julian spoke irrationally.

"What, you just gonna stay up all night?"

"Maybe."

"Julian, why don't you just call her?" Hoping that would sway his friend, Tommy recognized the uselessness of his suggestion. He watched the bartender chuckle and shake his head.

"Julian, you're doomed, so you might as well call her like Tommy here says."

Julian pulled out his cell phone in a dramatic gesture and turned it on to make the call. The cell phone showed he had missed a call. He punched the button to see who had tried to reach him. His screen read, "Private Number." Was that her? He listened to see if there was a message. There was none. Tommy, hoping to prevent his friend's spirit from taking a nosedive, dared Julian to make the call.

"Chicken. You can't make the call because you're whipped!"

"Oh yeah? Watch this." Julian took the bait.

"Only counts if you talk to her or leave a message," Tommy said, egging his lovestruck friend on.

The phone rang and rang and rang. Then Antoinette's voice came through the phone. It sounded like music to Julian's ears, even if it was only an answering machine. Then came the beep, beep, beep. Julian stood silent. "Come on, man, leave a message. Told you, he's a chicken."

Just to prove his best friend wrong, Julian began to speak. "Antoinette, it's Julian. Please pick up the phone." Silence. "Antoinette? Okay, you're not there, but I know you received the flowers I sent you. Please call me. Remember my number? It's 305-258-6088, I must see you." Julian hung up the phone and gave a gloating look to both Tommy and the bartender. The bartender bought the next round.

Ceci had listened to a voice leaving a message for Antoinette. It was Julian, and he was a wee bit drunk. Sensing that Antoinette had this man in a turmoil, Ceci sympathized with him. She also knew Antoinette. She'd never accept a person who was capable of getting drunk. Ceci made the decision to write the number down and delete the message. She'd contact Julian herself. Giving a second thought to her manipulation, she decided it was the right thing to do. *God forgive me.* She hit the button.

Antoinette couldn't believe the time had gone by so fast. She'd had a busy night. *The moon must be full,* she thought. And then she realized she hadn't even called Ceci. Thinking her unexpected guest was probably already sleeping, she gathered her things and left for home. Driving home, she realized she hadn't called Julian either. She still had to thank him for the flowers. *Odd,* she thought, *that I haven't heard from him since. He probably isn't serious. He probably just sent the flowers feeling bad about how our date ended. It had ended poorly and he hasn't called, so maybe I shouldn't even worry about it. Just a thing.* She pulled into her long drive. Her dark house and the lit porch light indicated that Ceci had already gone to sleep.

Quietly, Antoinette entered her house and saw Ceci sleeping on the sofa bed. Passing through the kitchen, she had the notion to check to see if she had any messages. There were none. Feeling slightly disappointed, she stripped for bed. Julian hadn't called and he wasn't serious. *Typical,* she thought. Maybe something really was wrong with her. Depressed, Antoinette turned off the lights and went to sleep.

Chapter 27

The Truth Sets You Free

Like fingers of smoke teasing her nostrils, the smell of bacon brought Antoinette into the morning. It was wonderful. She lay there listening to the clamor in the kitchen and realized how alive the house felt with more than one person being in it. Soft music joined the arousing aromas. Stretching, she looked at the clock and realized she had overslept; it was already 10:30 a.m.

Energized by the morning "wake-up call," Antoinette jumped out of bed and went into the kitchen, where she found Ceci outperforming Juan by making a marvelous breakfast spread. She gave Ceci a good-morning peck on the cheek and voiced her amazement. "My God, woman, who are you feeding, an armada?"

"A breakfast fit for a queen, dear. Good morning." The western omelet was placed on the platter next to a plate of fresh tomatoes and cottage cheese. Bread, yogurt, and OJ made it complete.

"Good thing. I'm starving!" The two women laughed and gathered around the table. Antoinette offered a quick blessing before sitting down and pigging out.

113

The two women planned their day, which would include a trip to Fairchild Tropical Gardens and then shopping in the Grove. Between bites, they agreed to end their day by having dinner with Sister Catherine.

Looking at the empty plate in front of her, Antoinette said, "Well, I think we can skip lunch after such a feast!"

Ceci smiled. It pleased her to see Antoinette so happy. "Well, there won't be enough hours in the day to finish all we planned if you don't go and get yourself dressed!" Antoinette pushed herself away from the dinette and went to get dressed while Ceci began to clean up.

"Just leave it, Ceci. I'll take care of it later," Antoinette called out from the bedroom.

"Don't be silly, child. When do you think you'll have time?" Seeing Ceci's logic, Antoinette consented. After a quick shower, Antoinette found her favorite T-shirt and a pair of blue jeans. Today was going to be a great day.

The sky was cloudless and the sun shone high and mighty, yet the temperature was cool with the winds coming in from the north. It was a picture-perfect day. The women drove down the long drive and were greeted by the clumsy pack of pups and the old mama dog keeping track of them from behind. Mrs. Griffin was sweeping her porch. Antoinette decided to stop for a moment to introduce her to Ceci. They declined the coffee Mrs. Griffin warmly offered, having had more than enough at breakfast. Antoinette explained their plans for the day, and Mrs. Griffin assured Ceci that the gardens were exceptional. Anxious to get on their way, Antoinette cut the visit short with a promise to come back later and tell of their adventure.

The drive up Old Cutler Road was nice, revealing beautiful homes with immaculately landscaped yards. Big old ficus, royal poinciana, and banyan trees lined the road, and bougainvillea were spotted everywhere in an array of colors. Antoinette slowed down and turned off into a shaded parking lot. They had arrived at the gardens. The parking lot itself was impressive with the tall old oaks that looked to have been a part of the landscape for a very long time.

Antoinette paid for their tickets. As they strolled into the park, Ceci could not believe the landscaping that opened up before her. "You haven't seen anything yet, Ceci! We'll take the train because the place is enormous." On cue, the little train pulled up and let off the tour group that took up most of the train. Ceci and Antoinette settled in the seats right behind the driver.

The driver knew his history of the botanicals very well and had a sense of humor. He pointed out all sorts of palms and trees and referenced their history. The few passengers were let off for a short while to walk through the emporium filled with orchids, bromeliads, and other exotic tropical and air plants. Ceci was in awe. Antoinette enjoyed her look of pleasure.

After piling back into the train, they were taken to the newest section of the estate. Here they decided to get off and make the walk back, waving goodbye to the other passengers as the train pulled out. "It's so beautiful, Antoinette."

"I know. I love the sense of peace you get here." They walked and spoke about many varied topics. Ceci took advantage of their remote solitude, the opportunity ripe to talk to Antoinette about her desire to marry and have children. "Somehow I guessed that you came to talk to me about something. That whole story about having business in Miami was a poorly planned cover-up."

"All right, I confess. But I felt it was very important that I talk to you in private about private feelings—at least to offer my experience as a woman, if you in fact want it." Antoinette was silent for quite some time, contemplating the offer. Ceci began to think she wasn't going to give her an answer.

"I can't do it," Antoinette finally said.

"I don't understand, Antoinette. What can't you do?"

"Leave my place of comfort."

Now it was Ceci's turn to be silent.

"Why?" The doctor began to pick through the words to uncover the emotion.

"Don't know, really. Fear, I guess."

"Physical or emotional?"

"Both."

"I see."

"Do you?"

Ceci stopped and turned to face Antoinette squarely. "How honest do you want me to be?" Antoinette was taken aback by Ceci's question.

"Why would I want you to be anything but honest, Ceci?"

"Because sometimes the truth hurts." Ceci was honest and frank. She continued to walk slowly at Antoinette's side until Antoinette was ready to answer.

"I am not sure I want to hear this."

"Then let me know when you are ready." Ceci just kept on walking. Antoinette couldn't stand Ceci's silent control.

"Okay, tell me, then."

"Antoinette, are you sure?"

"Come on, Ceci, now you are scaring me. Yes, I'm sure."

"Okay. Then let's find a place to sit, preferably in the shade. It is starting to warm up." Antoinette suggested they go back to the emporium where the orchids were housed. For the next few moments, they walked in silence.

They found a table in a shaded area. It took Ceci a few moments to figure out what words she would use. This was going to be a tender subject, but it was something that needed to be addressed if Antoinette were to move forward in her life. "When a person leaves a place of comfort, it means they are willing to risk the unknown for something they believe is the right course of action. Usually, people who don't leave their comfort zone refuse to do so because they don't know what they want. This causes them to miss out on the opportunities they may come upon. You, on the other hand, have just told me you can't leave your comfort zone because you are locked up in fear. Fear, my dear, is not a healthy emotion." Antoinette listened patiently, wondering where Ceci was going with this.

"Antoinette, you are an exceptional person. What you have accomplished in your life, you've done because you have a trait that many people lack: it's called self-discipline, and it is a form of control. This is what makes you a perfectionist and overachiever. Yet you only embrace those activities and relationships over which you have control. When I say control, I mean control over yourself, versus control of another person. Your so-called fear stems from your own inability to determine if the new experience you are going to face, in this case, a relationship, is something that will allow you to retain control over your own emotions. And do you know why you have such a strong need to maintain your self-discipline?"

"No, Ceci. And to tell you the truth, I never felt I controlled anything in my life," Antoinette stated, becoming defensive.

"Except your emotions, Antoinette. Do you remember why you came to the orphanage?"

Antoinette was silent and looked away from Ceci. Her friend was asking her to remember a part of her past that she had pretty much blocked from her memory. Why was she doing this? What did this have to do with anything? "I was abused by my father."

"Do you remember it?" Ceci knew the answer before Antoinette gave it.

"No, not really."

"Do you know why you don't remember it?"

"I guess I just blocked it."

"More than that, Antoinette. Because you could not control what was happening to you, you developed a second personality who did take control of the situation."

"That's the voice in my dreams?"

"Probably so." Antoinette felt like she had been taken out of reality and placed into a dreamworld. Deep down inside, she knew that Ceci was telling the truth—and she knew she didn't like hearing it.

"Antoinette, do you know what happened to your father?"

Antoinette didn't. As much as she tried to remember, she never could. And since no one at the orphanage would ever give her a straight answer, she just gave up. "No. And I don't really care."

"This is very hard for me to tell you, Antoinette, but I must because it is the root of your fear. The last time he attacked you, he hurt you very badly. You almost died. As a survival mechanism, you developed the second personality, what you understand to be a familiar voice. She was known as Sadie. Sadie took control over Antoinette and killed your father." *There, the worst part is over,* Ceci thought. Antoinette stared at Ceci. She didn't know whether she would go into a fit of rage or break down in tears. She was frozen.

"That is the extent of your control over your own emotions. Your fear of the physical part of a relationship is understandable, but if you don't want to remain a spinster, as you call it, all your life, then you must overcome your fear, take control of it so to speak. Your emotional fear of your relationship stems from the Sadie side of your personality. She is very protective of Antoinette. Yet you, Antoinette, must control Sadie. And in order to do this, you need to recognize that she still exists, that she is the root of this fear. You need to make decisions based upon what you feel in your heart and not because of the fear in your head." Ceci remained quiet while Antoinette digested the horrid truth of her past.

"Ceci, you have just told me that after being raped by my own father, I killed him because I have a split personality that took over—and this is the reason I fear a relationship." Antoinette reiterated what she'd thought she heard from Ceci.

"In a nutshell, yes, that's it."

Antoinette became angry. "Why, Ceci? Why did you tell me this?! What purpose does it serve me now? You should have left my past in the past." Antoinette stood and walked away after a very vocal public display of anger. She had just lost control. Ceci made a mental note of it.

Antoinette's head was spinning. She started to run, wanting to outrun Ceci's words and to regain control over her life. She ran almost three acres before she dropped and cried like a little child. She remembered everything, the pain and the shame. She remembered her mother, and her own loneliness when she died. She remembered her father's face just before she pulled the trigger. The images flashing in her brain were like a horror movie. Antoinette didn't care who saw her break down. She cried and screamed, releasing the anguish she had kept pent up for so many years. Her perfect world had just crumbled and she felt exposed.

The security guard, spotting Antoinette, let Ceci off at some distance as Ceci suggested. It hurt Ceci to see the pain Antoinette was suffering, but she knew it was necessary if Antoinette were to put Sadie away forever so she could get on with her life and establish normal, healthy relationships. Slowly, she approached Antoinette, who lay with her face to the ground sobbing. Ceci sat down next to her and placed a hand on her back, feeling it shake with each sob. Antoinette screamed in a muffled voice, saying how much she hurt, while Ceci did her best to remain calm and quiet by her side as Antoinette worked through her emotions. Ceci fought hard to hold her own tears back. She didn't know how much time had actually passed before Antoinette began to pull herself together. Antoinette looked at Ceci and began to cry again, clinging to her like a little girl. Ceci caressed her in the same motherly fashion she used to do when Antoinette was at the orphanage. She spoke quietly to Antoinette, explaining that what she was feeling was natural, and very good for her, as it would free her. Finally, Antoinette regained control over herself, wiping her face on her sleeve. All she could say was that she wanted to go home and go to sleep. Ceci got up, helped Antoinette to her feet, and walked her to the car.

Chapter 28

Julian awoke with a mother of a hangover. It reminded him exactly why he hadn't ever gotten really drunk after leaving college. He couldn't stand the nausea. Dragging his ill body into the kitchen, he grabbed two eggs and cracked them into the blender. After adding some tomato juice, he hit the blend switch. It was a nasty concoction, but it somehow always made him feel better.

He found his way into the bathroom and looked into the mirror as he relieved himself. What he saw was frightful. He looked like hell, not daring touch his face with a razor, at least not yet.

"What the devil happened last night?" he spoke out loud, struggling to recall the night before. He had been with his good ol' buddy Tommy. Julian had poured his guts out to his friend over several cocktails. Slowly, memories of the night's events came to him. "Oh God, what an ass I must have made of myself." He went to take a shower; water always worked.

Julian sat in the steamy shower for about an hour before he began to feel better. Letting the water run over his body, he thought about Antoinette and how she was turning his world upside down. "Bitch," he whispered, realizing she was the first person ever to have shaken his confidence. He needed to see her.

He knew he didn't have the nightmare only because he passed out. Was it true what Tommy chided him about? Was he really afraid of a commitment? Was his fear great enough to produce a nightmare? "Shit," he said to himself, "I can't even get a date in. Why the hell should I worry about a commitment!" That thought made him feel a whole lot better. "I'll give her one more chance, and that's it. Maybe she doesn't deserve someone as good as me." Wrapping a towel around his hips, he went into the next room to make the call.

Ceci had just tucked Antoinette into bed when the phone rang. "Antoinette, Antoinette! This is Julian! I've been trying to reach you. Didn't you get my message and the note with the flowers I sent?"

"Julian, hi. It's Ceci. How are you doing?"

"Ceci, hi … I'm sorry. I just assumed you were Antoinette. Is she there? Can I speak with her?"

"Julian, right now she's lying down. She's not feeling very well. But I've been meaning to call you myself. I need to speak with you. Can we meet for lunch tomorrow?"

"Ceci, is Antoinette okay?"

"Physically she's fine. But really—I'll explain everything tomorrow. Where shall we meet?" Ceci cut short Julian's line of questioning and agreed to meet him at a place called Mr. Moe's in the Grove. "Great, Julian. I'll see you tomorrow." Ceci hung up before he dared ask her another question.

She called Sister Catherine and canceled dinner, saying only that Antoinette was not feeling well. Sister Catherine understood; she always did somehow. Next Ceci called Juan to see how he was doing. She decided that she wouldn't give any details of the day until they were together.

"How are you, Ceci?!" Juan was happy to hear from his wife. It lifted his mood. Ceci disclosed only the best parts of their day and assured him that she was okay.

"Are you going to come for the weekend?" she asked.

"Yes! I can't stand for you to be away so long." That made her feel much better. They spoke for a few moments more. After hanging up the phone, Ceci decided that she too needed a nap. What happened at the botanical gardens had, in fact, been a very exhausting experience.

Julian held the phone in his hand, not sure of how he felt. Was something wrong with Antoinette? What it was he couldn't fathom, but at least he'd made a small step forward by making contact with someone in her family. He knew that Ceci and Antoinette weren't related by blood, but he had noticed a very strong bond between the two, particularly the day he'd asked Antoinette to go out to dinner with him. He remembered the event of the invitation and how abrupt and forceful Ceci was in overriding Antoinette's wishes. In any event, he knew that the next day would enlighten him somehow. He got dressed and spent the rest of the day running errands.

Chapter 29

Antoinette didn't come out of her bedroom until late the next morning. Feeling like she'd been hit with a sledgehammer, she nevertheless noticed the breakfast Ceci had made for her. Looking around, she also noticed that Ceci wasn't there. Truthfully, she didn't mind that. She needed time to herself. Going for the OJ, she spotted Ceci's note indicating that she was out running errands with Sister Catherine. Grabbing the plate Ceci had prepared for her and the glass of juice, Antoinette sat down to eat a quiet breakfast. The clock on the wall reminded her that she had to be to work in four hours. *Great.* She didn't feel like going anywhere.

Ceci had told her too much yesterday; she still didn't know what to do with it all. Yesterday, she had remembered everything, every single rotten memory of her past that she'd tried to bury. Having a split personality made her a nutcase, no matter how you sliced it. Sadie, that's what Ceci called her, was the root of her fear. An imaginary person Antoinette had created was preventing her from having what she wanted most in her life! She needed time to digest this information.

Antoinette continued to stare out the window. She loved the view from this vantage point, which was the reason she'd put the dinette there. It seemed to open things up in her tiny cottage. *Kind of like Ceci's talk yesterday,* she contemplated. It just kind of opened things up and threw the logic of her world into total chaos. But was that necessarily bad? "Comes a time," she whispered. The cat was out of the bag, so to speak; she had nothing more to hide. She could never go back to the day before yesterday, as Ceci's talk sealed that door forever. She was being forced to come out of her comfort zone, and it seemed scary as hell.

Antoinette's thoughts were interrupted by the sounds of Magic, who was making noise in the barn. She got herself dressed to go check up on him. Magic was all out of sorts, kicking the walls of the stall as if demanding to be let out. Antoinette looked at the other horse, Charlie, and noticed that he was acting like his normally calm self, except for an occasional laying down of the ears. Turning her attention to Magic, she could see his stress by the way he was breathing and behaving. She approached him carefully, singing him her usual sweet song while offering some oats. Refusing them, he kicked the door. He wanted out. As Antoinette opened the stall, Magic flew like a bat out of hell into the corral. But then the horse immediately settled down, probably because he'd been released. *Odd,* she thought. *Maybe he just needs to be ridden; he probably hasn't been properly exercised since the last time I rode, which was before I left for Naples.* Antoinette went to get the gear together so she could ride Magic.

Magic was Antoinette's favorite horse. It seemed to her that his behavior was simply the result of his spoiled-rotten self wanting attention. "Harrumph, you're just a spoiled brat, Magic! Okay, okay, let's go for a ride," Antoinette whispered to her friend, who walked with her down the drive, knowing the route. Antoinette liked riding outside the confines of the corral, as it gave her a sense of freedom. As she walked her old buddy south along the side of the road, drivers beeped their horns in appreciation, not realizing what a nuisance that gesture actually was.

Antoinette turned west off 147th Avenue toward the canal, the place where they could really run. Magic always seemed to relax after a good run; so did Antoinette. Getting back to nature always was a great way to relieve personal stress.

Looking at her watch once the ride was finished, Antoinette noticed that she had about two hours before she had to be at work, so she decided to start on her way back.

Antoinette was lost in her thoughts as she and Magic walked toward the cottage. She felt a sense of freedom after what had happened the day before. It was as if a pressure valve had released a lot of steam that had built up inside her. She hadn't noticed how much her pent-up emotions were hurting her. Maybe now she'd be able to have a relationship. Then again, maybe not. The thought of physical intimacy still frightened her. She thought of Julian and their kiss. That wasn't bad at all. Maybe she was wrong. "Oh, Julian!" she spoke aloud, remembering that she hadn't yet called him. "You must think I'm a snob!" She decided to hurry home and call Julian before she went to work. At least she could apologize for her bad manners.

Climbing back into the saddle, Antoinette said, "Ready for one more run, Magic?" He snorted his approval, and off they went. About five minutes into their ride, Magic sensed the danger and stopped suddenly, backing up nervously. "Whoa, Magic. What is it, boy?" Just then Antoinette saw what it was; a pack of wild dogs were fast approaching.

Magic began to buck as the dogs strategically surrounded Antoinette and her horse. She couldn't believe this was happening as Magic reared up in protective defiance.

In a flash, Magic and Antoinette were pushed back into the canal as the edge of the bank crumpled from their weight. She could hear her bone crack. The pain soared straight to her brain. She climbed back onto Magic, who was trying to gain his footing. Antoinette cried from the pain and fear. The dogs chased them along the bank, vicious and unforgiving, even trying to get into the canal. Luckily the dogs feared the water and were stuck on the north bank. If only Antoinette could get herself and Magic to the south side of the bank, but it was impossible, as the bank was too high. She couldn't get Magic out. Her leg was busted for sure, and God knows what else. The pain was fast becoming unbearable. Antoinette began calling for help. The next thing she heard was the sound of the sirens. Then she passed out.

Ceci, watching Julian come in, waved to him. He waved back in recognition, and greeted her with an enthusiastic hug once he reached the booth she was sitting in. He slid himself in, looked at Ceci, and bluntly asked, "How's Antoinette? And what's this all about, Ceci?"

"I like your straight-to-the-point attitude. And might I say that you look like hell?"

"Thank you. Now, what's up?"

Ceci smiled. Julian was showing all the signs of being head over heels in love.

"I'm here, Julian, to give you insight, an understanding so to speak, into what it takes to get close to Antoinette. However, this advice doesn't come free. It has its price, like everything else in life."

"Okay, what's the price?" Julian didn't like games.

"The price, Julian, is that you promise, before me and God, that no matter what, you won't hurt Antoinette."

"Ceci, of course. I would never do such a thing."

"Before you make that commitment, Julian, you must know that I am a retired psychiatrist, a person who has studied human behavior all her life, and particularly Antoinette's life. Think about what I just said. And excuse me for a moment while I go to the restroom."

Julian, bewildered, watched as Ceci walked down toward the restrooms. What the hell was she talking about? The minutes that passed seemed extraordinarily long to Julian. He began to brace himself for some terrible news. Just as a sensation of doom rested upon his shoulders, Ceci slid into the booth and began to speak her purpose. "So, Julian, can you make that promise?"

"Of course, Ceci. What is this about?"

"Antoinette is a very sensitive individual. She is an extremely talented person and very loving, and up until recently she was very much in control of her emotions. You see, Julian, I treated Antoinette at the orphanage she was sent to live in after she was severely abused by her father. Until yesterday, she herself did not realize all of this."

"Ceci, why are you telling me this? Doesn't it break some kind of client–doctor rule?"

"Julian, you are in love with a woman who loves you more than she herself realizes. I am here to ask for your cooperation." Ceci went on to explain in detail the events of the day before. "Julian, if you love her, and my guess is that you do—and that you are in denial about it—then you must know these things and be willing to accept them until you find the way to allow her to show her true feelings. Otherwise, Julian, I am asking you as a man, and a gentleman at that, never to make contact with her again. That is the price I am asking you to pay. Excuse me." Ceci answered her cell phone.

"Oh, hi, Sister. What? … When? … Where is she now?" Julian became immediately alarmed, worried that something terrible had just happened to Antoinette. "Julian, please, I need a favor. Can you rush me to Homestead Hospital? Antoinette has had a terrible accident while riding."

"Certainly, of course." Julian told her to wait at the door, saying that he'd bring the car around. In the meantime, Ceci called Juan.

Chapter 30

Ceci rushed into the emergency department's waiting room in a panic. Scanning the room, she spotted Sister Catherine praying the rosary. She took a deep breath and walked toward the nun. As Ceci was approaching, Sister Catherine looked up and saw her. She stopped praying and began to babble nervously about Antoinette's condition. Sister Catherine didn't handle stress very well. "Okay, Sister. Please slow down. Where is Antoinette?"

"In ICU under observation."

"Did you speak with the doctor?"

"No. I called you and have been waiting here since."

"Okay, Sister. You keep praying, please. I'll go find the doctor."

Just as Ceci was leaving the emergency department waiting room, she spotted Julian and motioned him to sit next to Sister Catherine, saying that she was going to find out where Antoinette actually was and what had happened. Julian looked in the direction of the nun, a heavy old woman bent over a rosary. She was obviously praying as she moved the beads through her fingers. He quietly sat next to her. Sister Catherine finished her prayers, wiped a tear from her eye, and blew her nose.

"Sister Catherine?" She struggled to turn to see the person next to her. "Are you Sister Catherine?" Julian asked.

"Yes."

"Hi, Sister. I'm Julian."

"The man who sent the flowers?"

"Yes." Julian was amazed that this woman knew he had sent Antoinette flowers. "How is she? What happened?"

Sister Catherine began to babble again, referencing a hostile horse, wild dogs, and canals. Julian was trying to grasp the situation. When Sister Catherine began to cry, Julian reached over and hugged her, hoping to calm her down. He wanted to leave this place and find out for himself what the hell had happened. Just then a physician came in asking for the parties waiting on Antoinette.

Julian jumped forward, leaving Sister Catherine behind to gather her old self together. *Where is Ceci?* he thought as he walked toward the doctor.

"Are you a relative of Antoinette Gonzalez?"

"Yes, I am her fiancé," Julian lied.

"Are there any other family members of closer relation here?" Just then Julian caught Juan searching the emergency room.

"Yes! Her father has just arrived," Julian lied again. Leaving the doctor for a moment, Julian called out to Juan and whispered into his ear, telling him to just follow his story. Juan's head was spinning. He was just about to speak his mind when Julian turned him toward the doctor and introduced him as Antoinette's father.

"Okay. Will you both follow me, please?" The doctor turned without waiting for an answer and headed down the corridor toward the ICU and Antoinette. They found Ceci there holding her hand and talking to Antoinette. "Is this the mother?" the doctor asked. Julian and Juan both said yes and then looked to each other. "Good. Ma'am, please come here so I can explain what is going on." Ceci left Antoinette and hurried to her husband's side, grabbing his hand. "Okay. First of all, she's going to live. The MRI indicates she has multiple fractures in one leg, a broken wrist, and a broken collarbone. No internal bleeding or punctures to vital organs, which is a miracle in itself. But she's pretty banged up and in a lot of pain. That is why we still have her in ICU. When the Xray department can get her in, we will set her leg. I'm afraid they are a bit backed up at the moment"

"Thank God," Juan said. Tears rolled down his face. The stress he felt on account of something life-threatening happening to his little girl simply overwhelmed him. Ceci hugged him, in complete comprehension of his emotion. She'd had a similar experience just before Juan and Julian arrived with the doctor. The doctor informed them that he'd be by later to check up on Antoinette.

Julian looked down at Antoinette. She was an angel, even with the bruising. In a deep, low voice, he called to her while grabbing her hand. "Antoinette, it's Julian." She moved slightly. "Antoinette, it's Julian. Please let me know if you can hear me." He felt her hand move. However slight the movement was, Julian knew that she was hearing him. Ceci motioned to Julian to indicate that she was going to take Juan to the waiting room, where Sister Catherine was. He nodded and then returned his attention to Antoinette.

Tubes and IVs ran everywhere. Her leg was twisted and black and blue. He could also see the dislocation of her collarbone. He winced imagining the pain. He was sure she had been given some form of painkiller.

Suddenly, the room was invaded by two nurses who announced that they were taking Antoinette down to get x-rayed. They ordered Julian to wait in the waiting area.

Julian sat next to Juan. Ceci had taken Sister Catherine home. Juan asked how Antoinette was, and Julian explained that she was getting x-rayed. "You'd think they would have done that by now." Juan was aggravated.

"It'll be a while, so all we can do is have a little more patience. Juan, may I ask you a question?"

"Sure, go ahead," Juan answered distractedly. He wasn't sure why Julian was there. All he knew was that the last time he was involved with Antoinette, she'd had a terrible nightmare. "What is it?"

"Did you know Antoinette's father?"

Juan was shocked by the question. "Yes. Who told you about him?"

"No one. I just wanted to know if you knew her father, Antoinette told me she was raised by the nuns in an orphanage. I know Ceci helped her as a psychiatrist. I just couldn't place your role in the whole picture."

"I was the one who found her," Juan truthfully answered. He couldn't wait to talk to his wife in private to figure out what was going on.

"Found her?"

"Yeah, after she killed the bastard." No sooner did he say the words than he realized that Julian in all likelihood didn't know the *whole* story.

Julian realized that Juan had stated more than he should have. Needing some time to put things into context, he excused himself from Juan. Apparently Ceci was a manipulator who told half-truths. In the hallway, he saw Ceci coming toward the emergency room waiting area.

"Ceci." She turned to see who was calling her and discovered it was Julian. "Ceci, I think you need to talk to me before you walk through that door."

"Yes, Julian. What do you know of Antoinette?"

"They are taking x-rays. How come you didn't tell me she killed her father?"

Ceci's blood ran from her face. "Who …?"

"Juan. He didn't realize you hadn't told me that part. I thought you should know that before you see him. I don't think he quite understands everything."

"Julian, I'm sorry …"

"Ceci, don't. Just let me be for a while." Julian, pissed about having been manipulated by this woman, needed a breath of fresh air. It was approaching 2:30 p.m. and he still hadn't had lunch. He went to the cafeteria to grab a bite to eat and figure out what he should do.

Paying the cashier and grabbing his tray, he acknowledged that the meal looked pretty good. He was hungrier than he thought. *Well, I finally got to see Antoinette again, but it wasn't how I expected it would be,* he thought, taking a bite from the hot turkey sandwich. She was pretty banged up and it was going to take some time for her to recover. He could walk away right now and never be missed. In a month he'd be leaving anyway. And then he'd never know if this was his once-in-a-lifetime opportunity to find true happiness.

Julian acknowledged to himself that it was Antoinette in the dream. Larger than life, she had turned his world upside down—and she probably didn't even realize it. Tommy was right; Julian was afraid of making a commitment. A woman like Antoinette required a commitment. And now he had the perfect opportunity to leave her behind forever. *Damn, forever was a long time.* He took another bite of his meal.

He thought about what Ceci, and then Juan, had said about Antoinette's past. He could only imagine what she must have gone through. Now he understood her reaction to their kiss, that intense moment when he was completely blindsided by the flood of passion that ran through him. *One simple kiss. Now it feels like she stole half of my soul. Why wouldn't she call me?* She'd completely ignored the three attempts he made to communicate with her. *Maybe she doesn't want to have a damn thing to do with me. Impossible,* he thought, *a kiss may be just a kiss, but the spark that's ignited is a whole different story. I should just walk away right now. But can I?* He turned his attention toward finishing his lunch.

Taking his last bite, Julian looked up to find Ceci and Juan standing before him. "They're resetting her leg and wrist now, and then she'll go back to ICU. They've got her pretty drugged, as you can imagine. She'll be heavily sedated for the night, so we are going to get my car and then maybe get some rest before we come back. I called her work just now. We understand if you don't stay. I want to thank you for bringing me here. I guess this is good-bye then." Juan hadn't said anything; Ceci had done all the talking. As Julian watched them leave, he was beginning to think she talked too much. She had given him another opportunity to just walk away. He got up and went to go see Antoinette.

Julian looked at her lying there. She was completely sedated. They had splinted her leg and wrist. She was lucky the fall hadn't killed her. He grabbed her good hand and gently caressed it. It too would be sore from all the needles poked in it. She was beautiful even now. He grabbed a lock of her hair and rolled it through his fingers. She was the woman in his dream; he mentally painted every detail of her face, ignoring the bruises caused by the fall. "Ah, my Antoinette, if only you knew how you've captured my heart," Julian whispered in her ear. Then he gently kissed her cheek.

"Julian," she whispered back faintly. At first, he thought he was imagining it, but then he saw her struggling to speak.

"Shh, Antoinette. Don't say anything now. Just rest. I'm here," he whispered. Then he kissed her temple. She went under again. He sat back in the chair and sighed, wondering what he should do. He began replaying in his head the last time they were together. He smiled remembering how beautiful she was. Her words played in his head: "Comes a time when we must leave our place of comfort and walk down new paths God has laid before us." Its meaning hit him like a freight train. At that very moment, his decision was made. He got up, whispered in her ear, kissed her temple, and left.

Chapter 31

The Path God Laid Before Us

One Month Later

"Antoinette, I won't go if you ask me not to." Julian held her hand and looked into her eyes. He was serious, vowing that he would do anything to keep her feeling safe, even if he had to refuse his biggest project ever. He had come to love her that much.

"Oh, Julian! Please sit down." She stared at the man seated before her. He had come into her life as an unknown knight in shining armor on a mission to rescue her. She smiled, more to herself, remembering how they first met. This same man had given her the first taste of passion. More importantly, he did not run away when she failed to give in. He was a man who accepted her past and who didn't leave, even when he was given every opportunity to do so. Above all, he was a friend who had come to visit her every single day, helping her pass the time while she recovered. She thought about this, about how close they had become over the past month, and about how much laughter he brought to her life. Now, he was offering to give up what he'd spent his entire career trying to achieve. What could she say?

"No, Julian. I am truly honored, but no. You must go and do your very best so the whole world knows who you are! This is the best gift you can give me. Besides, I'll be back on my feet in no time." She smiled and winked at him. He got up from his chair, placed his hands around her face, and kissed her slowly and fiercely. She caught her breath when he let go. God, she was going to miss him.

Collecting herself, she spoke as Julian gathered his things to leave. "Julian, I have one more question."

"Yes, my dear?"

"What made you stay?"

He laughed lightly. In his best French accent, he said, "*Mon chérie,* it was something you once said."

"Oh, pray, do tell!" Antoinette mimicked a perfect Southern drawl. He stopped what he was doing and turned to look at her directly.

"Comes a time when we all must leave our place of comfort and walk down the path that God has laid before us." She was awestruck. He blew her a kiss, grabbed his things, and walked out of the room backward, telling her he'd call her from New York. Antoinette closed her mouth and smiled. She felt loved.

About the Author

M.E. Rodriguez is a survivalist. She portrays this spirit in Empowering Antoinette by turning a woman's tragic beginnings as a young girl into a triumphant story of healing that gains the main character, Antoinette, an often sought reward: true love.

The author comes from a lineage of empowered women. An American of Cuban heritage, Ms. Rodriguez was raised in the Northeast of the United States. She was a member of the US Coast Guard Reserve and has a Master's degree in Business Administration. Professionally and for leisure, she has traveled extensively throughout Latin America, France, Spain, and the Caribbean. She speaks English, Spanish, and Portuguese.

Printed in the United States
By Bookmasters